THE LOVE OF HIS LIFE

"Would you like to go out sometime?" I asked.

She stared at me for a moment. "I can't."

"All right."

"I have a boyfriend."

"OK."

She smiled. "I'd really like to. You understand."

Sure, I understood a lot of things. It was amazing how intense my disappointment was. I couldn't believe it. I hardly knew her, I kept telling myself. I was never going to know her.

"How long have you been going together?" I asked.

"Two years. He's a great guy. You'd like him."

"Would *he* like to go out with me?"

She laughed. "You crack me up."

"I'm just one big bundle of laughs."

She quieted. "Thanks for asking. You're a nice guy, Mark."

Nice. I hated that word.

Christopher Pike

See You Later

AN ARCHWAY PAPERBACK
Published by POCKET BOOKS
New York   London   Toronto   Sydney   Tokyo   Singapore

AN ARCHWAY PAPERBACK *Original*

An Archway Paperback published by
POCKET BOOKS, a division of Simon & Schuster Inc.
1230 Avenue of the Americas, New York, NY 10020

ISBN: 0-671-74390-2

First Archway Paperback printing August 1990

10 9 8 7 6 5 4

AN ARCHWAY PAPERBACK and colophon are
registered trademarks of Simon & Schuster Inc.

Cover illustration by Brian Kotzky

Printed in the U.S.A.

IL 8+

For Rob

See You Later

===================== CHAPTER ONE

It began with a smile, or at least that's what I thought. But then, I didn't think much when I was eighteen. I just *longed* for things I didn't have, and *reacted* when they came to me and I no longer wanted them. But love . . . I always wanted to be in love, and to have love, and to pretend they were one and the same thing. I was like everybody else, I suppose, and I thought I was so different. I had to find that one girl who was so different, so perfect—who would accept me just the way I was.

I'm such a liar. I lie to myself constantly. The truth is I didn't know what I wanted back then. But when I saw her, I began to get an inkling.

She worked in a record store five miles from my house. I had been in the store a few times before but had never seen her. I love music. I had a compact disc player I had to scrape to buy and two hundred

CDs that made the plastic on my credit card peel on both sides. But I wasn't worried. I felt I could work my way out of any debt. In private I had tremendous self-confidence. The problem was outside my bedroom. There I was shy and awkward. When I opened the door to the record store and she spoke to me, I didn't know what to say.

"Hi," she said. "How are you?"

"What?" I asked. She was cute. I noticed that right away. But my heart didn't skip in my chest at the sight of her, even though I had been born with a congenital heart defect that caused my pulse to dance at the slightest provocation. It was not love at first sight. But I like to imagine that something did pass between us in that first moment, that destiny was at work. She continued to smile at me. Her teeth were white and straight, her eyes big and brown.

"I said, 'How are you?' " she repeated.

"I'm fine." I let the door close at my back, thankful for the air conditioning. Summer in Los Angeles didn't usually get off to such a fiery start, but that June was an exception. My car was like a furnace. "How are you?" I asked.

"Great," she said. "Can I help you find anything?"

"I'm just looking." I took another step inside. She was off to my right, behind a raised checkout counter; nevertheless, she was no taller than I was. I estimated her height at five two, her weight at a hundred even. I often do that—mentally record people's vital statistics. If a detective ever wanted to quiz me about the people present in any situation, I'd be ready. Her long dark hair possessed a remarkable shine. Her name tag read, "Becky."

"If you need help, give me a call," Becky said.

"All right." I surveyed the store. Except for one middle-aged lady, it was empty, which made sense. It was midday on a Monday, and school wouldn't let out for another two weeks. I was still officially a senior and waiting to graduate, but I had finished all my classwork by the January semester break. I doubted that I'd go back for the graduation ceremony. There had been only a few people at school I called friends. "Do you have a software department?" I asked.

"Yes." She pointed. "At the back, near the videos. Are you into computers?"

"I write computer games."

Her face brightened, and I asked myself if that was what I had been angling for—her approval. Ordinarily I don't brag to people about the computer games I've sold.

"Would we have any of yours?" she asked.

"It's possible."

Becky stepped down and out from behind the counter. "Let's see."

She led me to the software section. I walked behind her. She wore bright yellow pants and a short-sleeved shirt to match. For a few seconds I imagined what she'd look like in a bikini. She was on the thin side, but had enough curves to conjure up interesting images in my head. Still, she was just a girl. I was just a boy. I wasn't getting a crush or anything. It must have been the heat.

We stopped before the rows of games. Becky's store was part of a huge chain. The selection was excellent. I was happy to see they carried one of my games.

"What's your name?" she asked.

I pointed to the bottom row. " 'The Starlight Crystal.' "

"Is that German?"

I glanced over. I hadn't really been listening. She grinned and I felt foolish. "My name's Mark Forum," I said. "That one's mine."

She picked the box up and studied the cover, which I thought was dreadful: two space-suited jocks beaming each other with phallic-shaped ray guns. No one in the game even wore a space suit.

"You really wrote this program?" she asked.

"Yeah."

"I sold one of these yesterday," she said.

"Good. I can use the royalties."

"Do you get royalties?"

"Yeah," I said.

"How much?"

"Ten percent retail."

She was impressed. "You must be rich."

I shrugged. "I get by."

I just got by. By the time I'd received the five thousand dollar advance on my last game—I'd sold three so far—I was down to my last five dollars. I no longer lived at home. I'd decided to leave after my dad hit me over the head with a gallon vodka bottle minutes after he'd drained the contents. Fortunately, when my hair grew back, after the doctors took out the stitches, it covered the scar. The funny thing was, my dad and I got along great when he wasn't drinking. Three years earlier we'd had a wonderful day together. I used to wonder how my mother put up with him. Then she finally left, the day before my fourteenth birthday, to marry a fire-and-brimstone preacher. On the rare occasions when I saw my stepfather, he talked continually, raving on and on about how only Jesus could save him. And you know, I agreed totally. I accepted the fact that my mother preferred bizarre men. My home life was pretty pathetic.

"Are you still in school?" Becky asked.

"Not really. Are you?"

"I graduated at the semester," she said.

"So did I."

She continued to study the game. "Did you really write this?"

"Yeah."

"But it says a Tom Cleary wrote it."

"Tom Cleary is a pen name. There's a Mark Forum who writes computer games." I shrugged. "I didn't want to get confused with him."

"So what you're telling me is that you can't prove this is yours?"

"I wouldn't lie about it," I said.

"How do I know that? I don't know anything about you."

"What do you want? I.D. saying Cleary is the same person as Forum?"

"Yeah."

I was a bit taken aback. "I don't care if you believe me or not."

She laughed. "I was just kidding, Mark."

5

Again I felt foolish. "Tom's my middle name," I muttered. "My mom used to call me that when I was young."

"Do you know what my middle name is?"

"Becky," I said.

She touched her badge, nodding her approval. "How did you know it wasn't my first name?"

"You wouldn't have asked me to guess."

"You're quick. I always go by Becky."

"What's your first name?"

"I'm not going to tell you." She glanced at the blurb explaining the game on the back of the box. "What's this about?"

"It's a quest game. You travel around the galaxy looking for different crystals to make up one huge crystal that has the power to destroy all the evil in the universe. Along the way you get chased by wicked aliens."

"Is it hard to solve?" Becky asked.

"Not if you know one secret."

"What?"

"Do you have a computer?" I asked.

"No, but my dad does. What's the secret?"

"I don't want to ruin it for you."

She pouted. "Come on."

"Tell me your first name first."

"No," she said.

"All right, then—no clues."

She put the game back on the shelf. "If I buy it, will you sign it for me?"

"People sign books. They don't sign computer software."

6

She smiled. "You're difficult. Did anyone ever tell you that?"

"You're the first." I added, "I have extra copies of the game at home. Don't buy it. I'll give you one."

"Thank you, Mark."

That was the end of our first meeting. A girl came into the store right then and needed Becky's help finding a record by a group she'd just heard of. They were called the Beatles. The girl was younger than I was and was to be forgiven. I browsed for a few minutes before deciding to hit the road. I waved to Becky as I left. She waved back. Nice girl, I thought. That was all. I didn't want to marry her or anything.

My life. It had no direction. I wanted to do a million things: be a doctor, an astronaut, a writer. But I couldn't stand the thought of going to college. I couldn't forget how it felt to sit in class and stare at the clock and wait for the period to end so that I could go to my next class and do the same thing. I had no illusions about programming computer games for the rest of my life, at least not alone. Hardly a month went by before a new game came out that left the competition far behind, particularly as far as the graphics were concerned. I knew I was lucky to have sold the games I had. I didn't have the artistic talent to create fantastic scenes. To continue in the field, I'd have to go back to school and study my brains out, or else join up with a whiz partner, who in all likelihood wouldn't need me. I couldn't stand the idea of getting an ordinary job bagging groceries or making french fries. I hated to have a boss, to take orders.

Not quite eighteen yet and I was worried about my future.

Worried if I would have a future.

My health stunk. It was my heart. Walking up a flight of stairs made me gasp. Playing basketball or even catch turned me blue. I tried not to think about it, but it was like trying not to think of the fact that I had a body. Since I'd left home, I had only myself to rely on. I had no medical insurance. Naturally, both my parents knew about my problem; my defective aorta valve had been discovered when I was six. But whenever they asked—which was seldom—I told them I was feeling fine. And who knows? Maybe I was fine. I hadn't been to a doctor since I was sixteen. Maybe I had healed since then, I'd tell myself. What else could I do? The last cardiologist I'd seen tried to talk me into a new type of surgery that worked amazingly well on pigs. Getting sliced open and having someone stick his hands inside my chest didn't sit well with me, particularly when I saw that the surgeon who popped in after the cardiologist's explanation had a couple of nasty razor cuts from his morning shave. I told the docs I'd lay off the bacon and got the hell out of their office.

But listening to my heart making funny gurgling sounds as I lay awake late at night, I didn't know if my decision was right. My physical weakness had plagued me throughout my adolescence. I hadn't even had an adolescence—not really. The problems at home made it all but impossible for me to bring friends over. My defective valve ruled out sports. I went straight from being a young kid to being an adult. I knew I had a lot to be proud of, but I wasn't a man—not yet. Fighting to catch my breath in the early-morning hours before dawn, I sometimes cried for my mother.

But the night after I met Becky, I didn't wake once with chest pain. I dreamed of her. We were in a green place and we were happy. That's all I remembered. It was enough. The next day I promised myself I'd visit her again at the first opportunity. Unfortunately, I didn't get back to her record store for a couple of weeks, and she was off that day. The next two times I stopped at the store, she was off, too. A month after the day I had met her, I finally saw her again. By then I was an official high school graduate. I had gone to the ceremony after all, although neither of my parents attended—largely because I hadn't told them about it. I wasn't totally neglected, however. After they passed out the diplomas, I got a few hugs, a few kisses— many of the girls were already drunk. No phone numbers, though. I didn't go to the all-night party. I went home to sleep. I needed my rest.

Becky hadn't forgotten me. Her eyes widened the moment I came through the door of her store. She quickly came down from behind the cash register. She looked cuter than I remembered, even though I did remember her well. Her eyes in particular impressed me with their warmth.

"Who is Chaneen?" she asked immediately.

"The queen of the universe," I said. "Who else?"

Becky slapped her leg. "I knew it! Do you know how many hours I've wasted on your stupid game since I saw you?"

I was pleased. She had obviously bought "The Starlight Crystal" with her own money.

"None," I said. "Since playing one of my games is the highest activity a human being can aspire to."

She smiled. "You talk just like your characters. Is Chaneen's identity the big secret that you told me about before?"

"No."

"What do you mean, no? I have to be close to cracking it."

"You're not. It's impossible to make real progress until you know Chaneen's identity for certain. You still have a long way to go."

Becky thought I was putting her on. "How big is this game?"

"What's the last world you visited?"

"Neptune," she said.

"You've hardly warmed up your computer. You're not even out of the solar system. This game goes to the ends of the known universe."

She was impressed. "You must be a genius. Where do you get your ideas?"

"There's a place in Fairfield, Iowa. I send them ten dollars and they send me back three ideas."

She frowned. "Really?"

"I'll give you their address. They give out ideas for books and movies, too. For twenty dollars they send you complete outlines. All the big producers in Hollywood use them."

She laughed. "You're so full of it, Tom Cleary."

"Please, call me Mark. Tom Cleary doesn't exist."

She turned away, shaking her head. "I can't believe Chaneen is the big queen. Did you base her on anyone you know?"

"Not many girls I know can stop the sun from rising with a wave of their hand."

"You just don't know the right type of girl."

I thought the comment suggestive, and this time my heart did skip. It was only then that I began to realize I liked her—silly, I know, since I had already made four trips to the store to see her.

"It's hard to meet them when you work in your room all day," I said, trying to be suggestive myself.

"Where do you live?" she asked.

"Over the hill." I added, "By myself."

"Probably in a huge house, with all those royalties you collect."

"My apartment's small. I couldn't swing a cat in it."

"Do you have a cat?"

"No." I tried to think of something funny to say. That's my downfall when I talk to girls—trying to think. I'm fine as long as I keep my mind a perfect blank. Except that my face has a tendency to go blank along with my mind, and it's not that expressive to begin with. "I had a dog once."

"What happened to him?" she asked.

"He killed himself. He ran in front of a car on purpose."

"Right. Your dog committed suicide."

"It happens all the time. They just don't keep statistics on dog suicides."

"Why would he do it?"

I shrugged. "He couldn't break my game, either."

She punched me lightly on the arm. "You nut. Tell me the big secret or I might copy your dog. Then my death would be on your conscience."

"Tell me your first name first."

She took a step away. "No."

I summoned my courage from the depths of my soul. "Have some ice cream with me, then."

I had caught her by surprise. "When?"

"When you get your break."

She hesitated, for several seconds actually. The feeling created by our light banter vanished. "I can't take my break for another couple of hours," she said.

"It usually takes me that long to pick out a CD." An awkward moment followed. She didn't speak, didn't look at me. I added, "Don't you like ice cream?"

"Sure."

"We could go for frozen yogurt instead."

"I only get a fifteen-minute break."

I knew she was putting me off, but I persisted anyway. I'm not a pushy guy normally, and I wasn't that upset, I just figured I might as well give it my best shot. I didn't want to end up like my dog. He had always been afraid to take a chance with his life, except when it came to crossing streets. The story I told Becky was true, most of it.

"You can have any flavor you want," I said. "Mint chocolate. Bavarian chocolate. Chewy chocolate."

"Chocolate gives me pimples," she said.

"Hell, get vanilla, then. I might even pay for it."

She smiled faintly. "You're funny."

"Then it's a date?"

She nodded slowly. "In two hours. And you're not going to stay in the store the whole time. I won't work."

I agreed to her terms. I walked out of the store

12

feeling like a million dollars, my heart beating a million miles an hour. I didn't know why. She was obviously a klutz when it came to computer games. We obviously didn't have anything in common. It was as obvious as her big brown eyes. Boy, I thought, were they sweet. I hoped she didn't have a boyfriend.

I was back in exactly two hours. I had spent the time making up funny things to say. I actually wrote down several witty remarks on a slip of paper, which I stuffed in my pocket. But Becky was busy with customers when I returned. She kept me waiting another twenty minutes. I spent this time revising my witty remarks before I tore them up and threw them away.

Finally we went around the block for ice cream. Becky ordered one scoop of rocky road, which I tactfully pointed out had a ton of chocolate in it. I can't remember what flavor I had. It was cold, that's all I recall. We sat in a booth by the front window. Becky wanted to talk about my computer games. Her easy, flirty manner had returned, but she was evasive when I turned the questions on her. I wanted to find out more about her and began to suspect that she did, in fact, have a boyfriend. I considered asking her point-blank, but by then I'd decided to ask her out. I felt that even if she did have a boyfriend she might agree to go out with me if I didn't *know* she had a boyfriend. Not that she seemed like the cheating type, but, hey, she was human.

What was it about her that brought me to the point where I was willing to risk the ultimate humiliation a teenage boy can suffer—that of the big No? I don't know. She was cute, but so were a lot of girls, and never mind that most of them didn't go for ice cream with me on a regular basis. It wasn't her spunk that fascinated me either. Her allure was simpler. It was the way she touched me. Twice while we sat in the booth she reached over and tapped my bare arm. She did it to make a conversational point, but it had a deep effect on me, and once again, I didn't know why. The nerves in my arm didn't send a rush of pleasure exploding into my brain or anything silly like that. But the touch of her skin on mine felt good. It felt *right*. If I'd been bolder, I'd have reached over and touched her hand. But I didn't, and soon it was time for her to return to work. We climbed in my car and drove back to the record store. As she climbed out, she thanked me for the ice cream.

"I wasn't sure you were going to pay," she said with a smile.

"If you had ordered two scoops, it would have been a different story," I said. She stood holding the passenger door halfway open, ready to close it. A part of me kept saying to wait till the next time to pop the big question, while another part argued that I might not have the same opportunity. The last voice was the more persuasive. I didn't want to go home and spend the next two weeks kicking myself for not just asking her and getting it over with. "What time do you get off work?" I asked finally.

She hesitated. "Six o'clock. I have to take my mother shopping."

She might have been trying to head off my question, I realized. She was perceptive. Fortunately, I had no such problem. I sucked in a deep breath, let my heart pound a few times, and blurted out the question.

"Would you like to go out sometime?" I asked.

She stared at me for a moment. "I can't."

"All right."

"I have a boyfriend."

"OK."

She smiled. "I'd really like to. You understand."

Sure, I understood a lot of things. Life was a bitch. Life sucked. My insight into all matters of personal relationships was vast and unerring. I was a goddamn philosophical genius. It was amazing how intense my disappointment was. I couldn't believe it. I hardly knew her, I kept telling myself. I was never going to know her.

"How long you been going together?" I asked.

"Two years. He's a great guy. You'd like him."

"Would *he* like to go out with me?"

She laughed. "You crack me up."

"I'm just one big bundle of laughs."

She quieted. "Thanks for asking. You're a nice guy, Mark."

Nice. I hated that word. None of the football jocks in school had been nice. But they'd gotten the girls, oh, yes. I put the word *nice* right up there with "I like you as a friend" and "You have a great personality." I don't know, I wasn't bad looking. Looking in the mirror in the morning wasn't a painful experience. I had a nice friendly face, a lot of personality. Christ. Perhaps that was the problem, I thought. So many girls seemed to want guys who were going to be a problem. Sex and danger—they went together like peace of mind and insurance premiums. My hair was dark and curly, my eyes deep and intelligent. So I didn't have muscles? So I was underweight? So my heart always felt as if there was a weight on it? It was there inside my chest and beating. I felt things. I thought I felt a lot of things most guys never did.

"Well," I said finally. "It was fun while it lasted."

"You're still going to be coming in the store, aren't you?"

"Sure. It's a great store. I might try to get a job there."

"Not you. You're too good for that."

That was another thing about Becky that I had noticed from the start, something that had in fact given me the confidence to ask her out. She poked fun at me occasionally, but she had a curious respect for me, out of all proportion to my skill at constructing computer games. Not that it mattered now. I started my car.

"I'll see you around," I said. "Take care of yourself. When you're playing my game, you can get ahead best by looking behind."

"Is that the big secret?" she asked.

"No. It's Tom Cleary's."

CHAPTER TWO

My disappointment and embarrassment stung for a week. Then they began to fade, and when they were all but gone, I did the worst possible and most human thing. I drove back over the hill to visit Becky again. She looked great. She was happy to see me. We went for ice cream again. This time she didn't keep me waiting, and her answers were no longer evasive. She spoke openly of her boyfriend, when I asked. His name was Ray. He worked in a bookstore in a mall that was near her record store. He was a great guy. Yeah, yeah, I know, I thought. But I didn't know why I had asked. Curiosity, I guess. I wasn't thinking of killing poor Ray or anything.

I began to visit Becky regularly, twice a week, sometimes more. I bought more CDs than I could afford. I felt I needed an excuse to go into the store. Becky always gave me her employee discount—fifteen percent, which was pretty good if it was a CD I really wanted. I mean, she thought I had all these giant royalty checks coming in and that it was her job to recommend every blessed artist I might enjoy and that I would naturally want to take home. But I must admit she did have excellent taste. She turned me on to all kinds of new music. She was a musician herself, I eventually learned. She sang. But not professionally, only in the shower. I got a punch for asking when I could see her perform.

As time passed, I grew bolder with her. Occasionally I'd ask her out, sort of as a joke, sort of to stick the knife in a little deeper to see when my blood would start to bubble out. She would always laugh and change the subject. I loved the way she laughed, except when what I wanted more than anything else was a yes. Yes, Mark, you may not have the greatest body in the world, but you turn me on and I want to kiss you. Every now and then I would say mean things to her, hoping that they would make me appear sexier. But they were never that mean, and she never listened to them, anyway, and I'd be left feeling about as sexy as the cover of one of my computer games.

I can't say she lowered my self-esteem so much as she knocked it off its feet. Each time I saw her, I soared inside, but never too far off the ground, because I remembered I had crashed at takeoff. The relationship was cursed from the beginning. She had a boyfriend. Why was I chasing a girl with a boyfriend? I asked myself that frequently. You see, I had no illusions that I was *not* chasing her. I was still hoping that her boyfriend would suddenly disappear.

It was toward the end of summer, when I had known Becky about three months, that I met Vincent. We bumped into each other in Becky's store. It was a typical visit for me. I asked her out and she responded by inquiring how my latest game was progressing. Becky was very concerned that I was working hard and getting ahead. She took special pride in the fact that I could do something few people my age could do, and that she knew me. Unfortunately, at that time, the megabytes in my computer had swallowed my creativity whole. I would turn on my computer each morning and stare at the blank screen and pray for the invention of intelligent machines. I was stuck. I didn't know if my space heroes should go through a time warp or change clothes and try to defeat the local kung fu champ.

I happened to notice Vincent as I was leaving the store, just after I had said goodbye to Becky. He was standing in the software section. He had one of my games in his hand. I paused to see if he was going to buy it, and when he persisted in reading the back—apparently without coming to a decision—I decided to saunter over and say, "Hi! I wrote that game. Ain't I smart?" Actually, it wasn't ego alone that drove me. I often talked to people who browsed the software selections, to learn what they enjoyed. Market research, it's called. And if I did most of my research on pretty girls, that was Becky's fault.

There was something about Vincent that drew me to him besides "The Starlight Crystal" in his hand. He looked familiar. He was one of those people I felt sure I'd seen before, but it bugged the hell out of me because I couldn't remember where. His hair was longish and pale blond, and he had a few more muscles than I did, although we were about the same height. He looked up as I approached. His eyes were a piercing blue.

"Hi," I said.

"Hello," he replied. His voice was soft, his age a puzzle. He looked about my age, but the ease of his manner and his obvious self-assurance made him seem older. He nodded to the game in his hand. "You wrote this."

"How did you know?" I gestured to Becky. "Did she tell you?"

"Yes."

"When?" I had been talking to Becky for the last hour.

"An hour ago."

"You've been here all this time?"

"I wanted to talk to you," he said.

"About the game? Have you played it?"

"Yes. It's one of my favorites. You're very good."

I took pleasure in the compliment. "Thanks."

"I write computer games, too," he said.

"Really?" I was smart enough not to ask if he had sold any. If he had, he would tell me.

"Becky told me you think your graphics are weak," he said.

"It's true. They're very ordinary. You must have noticed."

"Yes."

I hadn't exactly wanted him to agree with me. "What's your name?"

"Vincent." He offered his hand. "You're Mark."

I assumed Becky had told him all about me. "Pleased to meet you, Vincent," I said, shaking his hand. "What kind of stuff do you like to do?"

"Science fiction. Fantasy."

"You're like me. You live around here?"

"Yes. Not far. I'd like to show you a game I'm working on." He hesitated. "Becky said you wouldn't mind."

I was surprised Becky hadn't mentioned Vincent to me when we'd talked. I didn't get a chance to ask her about it because at that moment she went into the back. I knew she had a ton of recently delivered tapes and videos to sort.

"Sure," I said. "I'll have a look at it. How far along are you?"

"I'm almost done. The major graphics are complete. I just have to decide what the major conflict is going to be."

"What?" I asked, amazed, thinking Vincent must be in more trouble than he realized. The plot of a game had to be thoroughly developed and charted before the first lines of code could be written. Otherwise, the amount of time wasted on a wrong turn could be staggering.

"I'd appreciate your input," he said calmly.

"No problem." He struck me as safe enough. "I'm free right now. Do you want me to follow you to your place in my car?"

"If you would." He put the game back on the shelf. "I already have a copy of this at home."

"Vincent? Have we met before? You look awfully familiar."

He hesitated. "I come into this store a lot."

I chuckled. "To see Becky? I do. She's a great girl."

He smiled, a smile as soft as his voice. "I have a girlfriend."

Outside in the cool night air, I stopped worrying about whether or not Vincent was in trouble with his game. He drove a black Testarossa Ferrari, one of the fastest cars on the road. Following him in my twice-rebuilt Toyota, I figured that if I had a car like his, I could sell it and live comfortably for the next ten years. Or afford heart surgery and maybe be dead in ten days.

Vincent had his own place. I was impressed. We parked in a circular driveway and walked to the front door. The house itself wasn't spectacularly huge, but it was perched on top of the hill I crossed whenever I went to Becky's store. It had a wonderful view of the city lights far off. Also, the landscaping was exquisite; even in the shadows of night, I could see that the bushes and trees were well groomed. The fragrance of blooming roses filled the air. I envied him his side yard. One could take it straight into the hills and disappear. Despite my heart, I still enjoyed a good walk. A good slow walk.

"You really live here alone?" I asked after he told me the house was his.

"My girlfriend stays with me," he said, opening the front door without a key.

"Is she here now?"

"She'll be along later. If you stay, you'll meet her."

We stepped inside. I was surprised to see that the house had very little furniture. A couch, a bar, a chair, but no TV or dining room table. Aside from the lack of furnishings, the house felt distinctly unoccupied. Vincent must have sensed my thoughts.

"I haven't been here long," he said.

But he had been visiting Becky's store for a while, I thought to myself.

"Did you grow up in Los Angeles?" I asked.

"Yes."

"Your family must have money."

"Yes." He gestured toward the kitchen. "Let me get you something to drink. What would you like?"

I shrugged. "A Coke, if you have it."

"I do."

We sat at the bar and drank Cokes together, enjoying the view of the city lights. I quickly discovered that unless I spoke, Vincent would lapse into silence. Briefly I wondered if he did drugs, but he betrayed no hint of dullness. His blue eyes were remarkably shiny. I didn't feel in the least uncomfortable around him even when he was silent. He was one of those rare people who was in absolutely no hurry to have anything happen. I had to bring up the matter of his game. Nodding and carrying his drink with him, he led me to his bedroom. Here again the furniture was sparse. A mat on the floor took the place of a bed. He had no chest of drawers, and a glance into his open closet told me he didn't own many clothes. But his computer was excellent, top-of-the-line. Although I made my livelihood on a computer, all I had was a clone of his. I had picked it up at a swap meet. He gestured for me to have a seat in front of the screen and flipped on the machine.

"Is this your first crack at programming a game?" I asked as the computer did a RAM test.

"No. I've done several games."

"Do you have any here?"

"No," he said.

"Why do you want to program games? You obviously don't need the money." I didn't imagine for a moment that he had paid for his Ferrari with software royalties. If he had, I would have heard of him. Then again, he hadn't told me his last name.

Vincent pulled up a chair beside mine. "I enjoy it. The games are excellent educational tools."

"I think most people just play for fun."

"You can learn while you're having fun," he said.

"Are you trying to teach something in particular?"

"You tell me after you've seen what I've done."

He had a color monitor. The password for loading his program was "Vincent." He took me right into the game, not into the code, which would have made no sense to me without several hours of study. Some days my own code was incomprehensible to me. The screen brightened with the smartly lettered title: "Decision."

"Interesting title," I said.

"Do you like it?"

"Yes, I like it. But I don't think it will sell. Forgive me for being blunt. I assume you want my honest opinion."

"I do," Vincent said. He was observing me closely to see my reaction to his creation. But he wasn't the least bit anxious. I pressed a key, and a clearly defined and wonderfully drawn space station filled the screen. It was revolving with such real-life precision that I could hardly imagine the hours he must have spent to achieve the effect. I marveled at his skill. I had never seen anything remotely approaching his graphics—outside a movie theater, that is. It was only after a few minutes that the reason for his sophisticated graphics dawned on me.

"What is the RAM in this computer?" I asked. The RAM, or random access memory, determined how much space the computer had to work with at any one moment. The greater the RAM, the more exotic a program could be.

"A megabyte," Vincent said.

"But this game will run on a lot lower RAM, won't it?"

"Does it matter?" he asked.

"You can't be serious? How do you expect to sell it if only one in ten machines can run it?"

"I'm not worried about that right now. I just want to create the finest game I can."

"All right," I said, already thinking Vincent was hopelessly idealistic. "What's the game about?"

Vincent pressed a key, and the earth—also beautifully drawn and defined—appeared below the space station. An instruction box in the upper right-hand corner immediately informed me of the space station's armament: neutron beams, helium lasers, three hundred missiles tipped with five nuclear warheads each and packing a ten megaton punch. We were obviously talking Star Wars here, SDI—Strategic Defense Initiative. I must admit I was disappointed. I had hoped Vincent's imagination matched his artistic vision. Nuclear war games bored me to tears. There were too many of them on the market. I mean, how many times could you blow up Russia?

Then I saw that the enemy was China. It made more sense, in a way, because of the speed with which our relationship with Russia was improving. Since the game was set in the future, it was reasonable to believe that China had advanced to the point where it could take on the United States.

"The United States and China are on the verge of war?" I asked.

"The whole world is," Vincent said.

"What's the goal of the game?"

"To win."

"Obviously, but what's your problem? Do you have a second space station in orbit? One belonging to the Chinese?"

"I've only got the one."

"Right off, I don't think that's a good idea. Say the entire earth gets obliterated. It would be nice for our heroes in the space station to have a final enemy to face."

"I was trying to be realistic," Vincent said.

"You can have two space stations and be realistic. The game's far in the future. The Chinese are as smart as us. You could use ninety percent of the same code you've written for the American station to create the Chinese one."

"I'd just like there to be the one."

"All right." I could already see he wanted my approval rather than my advice. But he didn't seem put off by my suggestions.

I pressed the next key. Immediately I was called upon to make a decision. Diplomatic solutions had failed, and negotiations had broken down. Both sides were readying their missiles for launch. My options were numerous: I could fire my lasers and destroy the Chinese missiles in their boost phase; I could try to take out Chinese subs off the west coast of the United States with my neutron beams; I could send a barrage of missiles down on the major Chinese cities. After playing for a few minutes, I learned that I was limited to one option at a time and that for each measure I took, a countermeasure was taken by the enemy. For example, if I fired *three* missiles, *nine* Chinese missiles would be hurled toward the United States. The discrepancy in numbers made sense because, I did, after all, get to make the first move. Now I could let the nine missiles hit the United States and concentrate on taking out more Chinese cities and subs, or else I could try to protect my country as well as the space station. I only had to play the game for a short time to realize that I—sitting inside the space station—was a primary target.

Scene after scene, the graphics of the game were exceptional. The logic of attack versus counterattack was also impressive. Vincent must have studied the theory of modern warfare in depth. At least I thought so at first, but soon—too soon—the game became unmanageable. Too many things were happening at once. I couldn't keep up. Also, countries that hadn't even suffered direct hits were being totaled up as casualties. I stopped to protest.

"What the hell happened to Australia?" I asked.

"It's dead," Vincent said simply.

"Why? Melbourne and Sydney haven't even been touched."

Vincent pointed to the total number of megatons that had been detonated. It was well past the ten thousand mark.

"Billions of tons of dust and smoke have been forced into the atmosphere," he said. "The greenhouse effect is now a certainty. The earth is going to freeze."

"That will take years."

"True. But Australia will be dead before then. The dust and smoke are radioactive."

"But that's ridiculous. You can't have a game like this. You should only focus on war day. No one can possibly win if you have to take into account factors like radioactive dust. The only ones who'll be left are the people on the space station."

"That's the problem I need your help with," he said.

"Just dump this radioactivity and greenhouse garbage."

"But I want the game to be realistic."

"That's noble of you," I said. "But you lose any possibility of a goal. No offense meant, but the player can't win this stupid thing." I paused. "Unless you've set it so that China can be knocked out quick and clean."

"I haven't."

"Then do that if you feel you have to keep it realistic. Also, you've got to put up a Chinese station. It's just not fair that our side should be the only one with weapons in space."

"Could you help me make it work?" he asked.

"What?"

"Could you help me?"

"No. I mean, I'd love to, but I'm busy. Anyway, I don't think you need my help." I gestured at the screen. "I can't create scenes like this. You're talented. Fix this thing up so that it makes sense and get it to run on a lower RAM, and a major computer software house will give you a six-figure advance easy. Really, I'm envious."

"I'll split the advance with you," he said.

"Get off it."

"I'm serious."

I chuckled. Then I looked at his face and stopped. He was watching me intently. He meant it. But I didn't feel I was being pushed into a decision. Quite the reverse, I had the feeling he was trying to help me. Half of a six-figure advance would be a lot of money to me.

I didn't get a chance to answer him. I heard someone come in the front door just then. Vincent stood and called out, "Kara?"

"It's me, it's me." A cheerful English accent sounded down the hall. "There's a car outside. Do we have guests?"

"Just one," Vincent said. "Mark Forum is here."

Kara entered the room. I tried to stand, but I misplaced my legs when I saw how pretty she was. Like Vincent, she was blond and blue eyed, but there the similarity ended. Vincent was calm almost to the point of serenity, but Kara obviously was charged. At the sight of me, she went up on her bare toes and pressed her palms together in a soft clap. Her face radiated pleasure.

"Is this the computer genius you told me you were trying to find?" she asked Vincent, keeping her eyes on me. I'm ashamed to say I forgot all about Becky at that moment. Kara's hair fell past her waist—a mass of tiny golden curls that clung to her like a warm embrace. Her mouth was wide. As she smiled, her red lips parted, revealing perfect white teeth. She seemed so delighted to see me, a complete stranger, that I didn't know how to react.

"This is him," Vincent said.

I turned to Vincent. "You were looking for me at the store?"

He nodded. "Becky told me you came in regularly."

Kara stepped farther into the room, her hand extended. I finally managed to get to my feet. She nodded to me, and I took that to mean I was doing fine. I felt as if I were being tested, but that was OK because I was passing with flying colors. I felt an immediate sense of ease and familiarity with Kara as I had with Vincent. Yet Kara looked and sounded like no one I had ever known. Her hand was cool and soft, her grip firm.

"I'm pleased to meet you, Kara," I said.

"Vincent showed me your games," she said. "They're clever. I was hoping he'd find you."

I shook my head. "I can't believe I'm so popular."

"In a select group," Kara said and glanced at her boyfriend.

"I was just showing Mark my game," Vincent said.

"Do you like it?" Kara asked me.

"Yes, I do. Very much."

"But it needs work, huh?" she said in a slightly teasing tone. It was strange, but I didn't know if she was teasing Vincent or me.

I shrugged. "I think a few changes would give it more commercial appeal."

Kara moved to Vincent and wrapped an arm around his shoulder. She kissed his cheek. "Can you help my big boy?" she asked me.

"Sure," I said. The word was out of my mouth before I realized it, but I had no regrets. I found them both fascinating. "But I couldn't possibly accept half your advance money, Vincent, if we get that far."

"Whatever you think is fair will be fine with me," Vincent said, raising his head. He had lowered it the moment Kara came into the room, almost as if he wanted my first meeting with his girlfriend to be private.

"Let's see how much work I actually do," I said.

Kara laughed easily and tossed her head, and as she did so, her long yellow hair rippled like small sunlit waves. I was romanticizing her, it's true. I did envy Vincent for having her as his girlfriend, but I wasn't jealous of him. Becky returned to my mind, and I was content with my thoughts of her.

"Now that we have that out of the way," Kara said, "what are we going to do next?"

"Do you want to work on the game?" I asked Vincent.

"I don't care," he said.

"Would you mind going for a walk and eating ice cream?" Kara asked, not waiting for an answer. "This is no time to work. It's time to get to know one another. Let's go for a stroll under the stars and stuff our faces."

Apparently Kara wore the pants in the relationship, although she had a dress on at present, a loose knee-length skirt that showed off her shapely legs. Whenever I think of Kara, I see her spinning around me in a short dress, brimming with enthusiasm and grace. Vincent never did answer her, except to lower his head again. It was decided. We would go for a walk and eat ice cream. It was what Kara wanted.

Kara had brought ice cream home with her, three pint containers, softening on the kitchen table. She handed us each a spoon, one for each of the three different chocolate flavors. She obviously wasn't worried about pimples, as Becky supposedly was.

We left by the side door, eating our ice cream, and stepped onto a path that led straight into the hills. It was a dark night, moonless, but I was able to distinguish the grade of the slope. I was worried I would quickly become a burden to the expedition. There is something about climbing that is particularly hard on heart patients, and I hated to admit to Kara and Vincent what a weakling I was.

But the admission proved unnecessary. Kara stepped off the path so frequently to collect flowers or to investigate croaking frogs that I was given frequent breathers. Vincent was obviously used to her behavior and didn't hurry her along. It took us half an hour to walk three-quarters of a mile into the hills. Rounding a bend in the path, we saw the city lights stretching for miles into the distance on our right. Vincent raised a hand to stop us and stepped off the path. He disappeared into the very side of the hill.

"What the hell," I muttered.

"There's a cave," Kara said quickly. "Vincent and I often come here. He keeps a telescope inside."

"Is that safe? Someone might find it and steal it."

"Unlikely," she said. "The opening to the cave is well hidden. Even in the daytime you'd probably walk right by it."

"But Vincent said you only just moved here. How did *you* find it so easily?"

"Friends told us it was here," she said, moving to the edge of the hill and looking out on the city. The hillside was mostly gnarly shrubs and dead grass, with an occasional tree bent over and waiting for rain. The air was still, the dry heat disturbed only slightly by faint damp undercurrents that hugged the ground.

Kara sucked in a deep breath and let out a happy sigh. "This is so neat."

"It's quite a view," I agreed. "Where are you from?"

"Don't you recognize my accent?"

"It sounds English."

"It's Scottish, actually. But I've lived in this country so long, I'm losing my accent. Or gaining another one, depending how you look at it."

"How did you and Vincent meet?"

"The way everyone does."

"Which is?" I asked.

"By chance."

"I'm serious."

"So am I," Kara said and giggled. "Do you have a girlfriend?"

"No."

"No?"

"Well, there's this girl I like. But she has a boyfriend."

"What's her name?" Kara asked.

"Becky. She's the girl who told Vincent about me."

"She works in the record store?"

"That's her," I said. "She's neat."

"If you like her, go after her. Don't worry about her boyfriend. How much do you like this Becky?"

"I don't know, she's neat."

"You're repeating yourself. Sounds like love to me, Mark."

I was embarrassed. I couldn't believe I was discussing Becky, I hadn't even written about her in my diary. I was waiting until I had some good news to report.

"I've asked her out," I said. "I asked her out a few times."

"What did she say?"

"No."

"No means nothing. Does she get angry that you keep asking her?"

"No. We've become friends. She's very sweet."

"She's interested," Kara said. "Take my word for it. I'm a girl. If she wasn't, she would have told you to take a hike by now."

"I don't know. She could just be acting polite."

"What's her boyfriend do?"

"He works in a bookstore."

"What's his name?" Kara asked.

"Ray."

"Do you know which bookstore he works in?"

"Yes. Why?"

"Have you ever gone in to see him?"

"No," I said. "Why would I do that?"

"To see what you're up against."

"This isn't a competition."

"Sure it is. Don't fool yourself. Love is like everything else in this world. You have to fight for it. Look, do want my help?"

"Your help?"

"In getting Becky."

"Kara, I don't mean to be rude, but I hardly know you."

"This will be a good way for us to get to know each other."

"Isn't getting a girlfriend something I have to do for myself?"

"Why should it be?" Kara asked.

I stopped. "Why do you want to help me?" I asked.

Kara stared at me for a long moment. I was wondering if I had insulted her with my question because she didn't respond. Finally, however, she broke into a smile and fluffed up my hair with her hand.

"Because," she said.

"Because what?" I asked.

She took her hand back. "Just because."

The spot where Vincent was now setting up the telescope offered an unobstructed view in all directions. I could see that Vincent spent as freely on his optical equipment as he did on cars. He had a ten-inch Schmidt-Cassegrain, a telescope that twice folded the light collected by its primary mirror—a favorite of wealthy amateur astronomers the world over. I had always had a special interest in astronomy, but lack of funds had stopped me from seriously pursuing the hobby. Plus L.A. was no place to look at the stars. City lights and smog had done away with the Milky Way years ago.

"Can we look at the moon?" Kara asked as Vincent fiddled with the eyepieces after the tripod was set on a flat portion of the path.

"It isn't up yet," he said. "It's three days past full."

"But it'll be up soon," I said. When the moon was full, it rose in the east close to the time the sun set.

"I know," Kara said to Vincent, almost in apology.

"We'll look at the planets," Vincent said.

"You really should take this thing out to the desert where the air is clear," I said, not sure what the big deal was about the moon.

"We like this spot," Kara said. "Hey, can we see Becky's record store from here?"

"Kara," I said.

"It's just about eleven. Maybe we can see Becky getting off work," Kara went on. "We could see her walking out to her car." She laughed. "We could use *high* magnification."

"We can't see the store from here," Vincent said softly, bent over the eyepiece and fiddling with the focusing knob. "Come here, Mark. I want to show you something."

"What is it?" I asked, moving a step closer.

"The space shuttle," Vincent said.

"*What?*" I gasped. "How could you locate the shuttle?"

"It's in orbit," Vincent said.

"I know that," I said. "But I would think it would take hours to find."

"It's not that hard if you know where to look," Vincent said. He gestured to the eyepiece. "Take a look."

It took me a moment to get my bearings as I pressed my eye to the ocular. Vincent was using low magnification; the field of view was large, dense with stars despite the interference from the city lights. In the upper right-hand corner, a bright white star was moving steadily across the star field.

"How do you know it's the shuttle?" I asked.

"If it isn't, then it's a flying saucer," Vincent said. "Do you want to look, Kara?"

"No," she said.

"Take a look," I said, fiddling with the knob. I was attempting to elongate the point of light, trying to make it look like the shuttle I was familiar with on TV. I realized that was probably foolish without a major observatory's telescope.

"You two look," Kara said.

"It's moving out of the field of view," I told Vincent.

"Let me help you," he said, putting his hand over mine on the focusing knob. He pressed his face close to my nose in order to peer through the tiny finder telescope strapped to the side of the main instrument. The walk up the hill must have taken more out of me than I realized. Suddenly the entire star field blurred, and Vincent hadn't turned the focusing knob. It was me: my eyes, my blood, my damn heart. A wave of dizziness swept over me and I staggered back. If Vincent hadn't caught me, I would have fallen. The irregular beating of my heart often made me dizzy, but this was stronger than anything I had ever experienced. Vincent led me to a nearby boulder, supporting me with both arms, and helped me to sit down.

"Take long, deep breaths," he said.

I followed his advice, keeping my eyes closed. It wasn't long before the spell passed. A minute later I felt fine, although a bit foolish. If Kara hadn't been there, it wouldn't have been so bad. Showing weakness in front of a girl always embarrassed me. As I looked up, I found her kneeling anxiously by my side.

"Are you OK?" she asked.

"I'm fine." I chuckled. "It must have been something I ate. Really, I'm perfectly all right. It was nothing. What were we talking about?"

"Space," Vincent said. He knew it wasn't something I ate. But he didn't question me further because he also knew I didn't want to talk about it. So did Kara. As suddenly as the dizziness had come, so also came a rush of love for both of them, mysterious and illogical in its origin. They were both strangers, I told myself. Yet, already they were my friends.

We spent the remainder of the evening surveying the sky and eating ice cream. I suffered no further attacks. Saturn and Jupiter were both visible. Unlike the shuttle, the planets seemed to interest Kara, and she had no qualms about looking at them. We also searched for and found a number of globular clusters and nebulae. Vincent was skilled at plotting sidereal coordinates. He would look them up in a small reference book he carried—the telescope had a small red light attached that allowed him to read—and know where to aim the telescope after only a minute of calculations. He was so obviously my mental superior that I felt silly even thinking about helping him with his game. I asked him if his interest in astronomy had inspired his computer game. He said, "Indirectly," but didn't elaborate.

Sometime after midnight we took down the telescope, and Vincent returned it to its place inside the cave. I was curious to see the cave for myself, but Kara said to wait until daytime, or until we had a flashlight. I didn't get the impression they were hiding anything from me.

We parted in their driveway; I didn't go back into the house. Vincent gave me his phone number and told me to call him whenever I wanted. He shook my hand and left me alone with Kara. She walked me to my car.

"I'm glad you're helping Vincent with his game," she said.

"I just hope I don't screw it up," I said.

"I'm sure after you play it for a while you'll know what to do."

"We'll see." I opened my car door and got in behind the wheel. Kara stood to my left, slightly behind me. A breeze had come up from farther down the hill. It lifted her long hair and floated it behind her, creating the impression that she was wearing a cape made of gold. She seemed pleased to have met me, but unlike Vincent, she seemed to have a lot on her mind.

"I want you to think about what I said," she said.

"About Becky?"

"Yes."

"How could you possibly help me?"

"I'm full of ideas. Do you want me to tell you some?"

"No," I said. "Becky's happy with who she's got. I have no right to interfere."

Kara looked down at me. She was no taller than Becky, but she gave the impression of great stature. She didn't have Vincent's calm confidence, but she had something few girls her age possessed—a sense of mystery.

"Are you sure?" she asked.

"That I shouldn't interfere? Of course."

"No. That she's happy. How do you know? Have you ever asked her?"

"It's none of my business," I said.

Kara leaned over and kissed me on the cheek. Her lips were warm, her breath cool and sweet like chocolate ice cream.

"You're wrong, Mark," she said.

CHAPTER THREE

The next evening found me back at their house. Vincent welcomed me warmly. Kara was out. When I asked Vincent where she was, he smiled faintly and said she was impossible to keep track of. I was disappointed, but only slightly. Vincent was excellent company, even if he spent most of his time with his mouth closed. Maybe that was what made him easy to be around. He had to be the world's greatest listener.

Except when it came to his game. He didn't reject my suggestions so much as he ignored them. At present, he said, he'd be happy if I simply played the game and learned how it worked. This made sense, up to a point. It was true one had to play a game for many hours, weeks even, to get a complete picture of its logic. But the major problems I had discussed with him the previous day were not going to disappear with an in-depth analysis. I told Vincent this, and he nodded—I had to assume he heard me—and that was the end of it. Then, at his gentle insistence, I played the game once more.

"Decision" both frustrated and intrigued me. The manner in which the enemy responded to each of my attacks was a lesson in cause and effect. The more elaborate my attack, the more clever the countermeasure. Playing the game, there was usually a point where I'd get a rush of adrenaline, my heart would pound, and I'd think, "I'm going to beat these bastards! I'm going to win!" But, of course, that was the problem. I couldn't win. No one could. The earth would be as good as dead before I could really get down to business. I never even got a chance to use all my missiles.

But I didn't get bored. I had a goal, one that I thought was achievable even with Vincent's current programming. So the earth got wasted, I thought. If I could finish a game with the space station intact, I felt I would have beaten it. Then I would feel justified in making Vincent rip into his code. "See?" I would say. "The operation was a success, but the patient died."

In the next two or three weeks, I visited Vincent five more times. Kara was present on all but one occasion. She would greet me at the door, usually in shorts and a T-shirt, and get in as much conversation with me as she could before Vincent would appear and we'd retire to do battle with the forces of evil. Our friendship deepened steadily. Kara and I talked about everything: music, the environment, politics. Kara was extremely liberal, very down on the military. I understood why she didn't want to look at the space shuttle. It seemed to her that every other shuttle put a new spy satellite in orbit. For the sake of our discussions, I would try to present the opposite argument— the need for a strong defense. Kara would hear none of it. She was stubborn. For his part, Vincent would only listen patiently to whoever was talking and then politely ask where we should go for ice cream.

I decided Kara had forgotten about Becky; she hadn't raised the subject since the first night. But at the end of my seventh visit, when we were waiting for Vincent to shower so we could go out, Kara suddenly brought up Ray, Becky's boyfriend.

"I've been to his bookstore a few times," she said.

"What for?" I asked, surprised.

"To see if he's half the man you are."

I admit I was curious. "Is he?"

Kara made a face. "He's a jerk."

"What makes you say that?"

"He tries to pick up every pretty girl who comes into the store."

"You're just saying that."

Kara reached over and took my arm. "Come on. I'll show you."

"What? I don't want to see him."

Kara pulled me to my feet. "You're going to see with your own eyes how miserable he's going to make Becky unless you stop him."

"Right now? What about Vincent? We can't just leave."

"Vincent won't care. Nothing bothers him."

"This is crazy."

44

Kara stared me in the eye. "Are you afraid?"

"Of what?"

"Becky?"

"No. It's not Becky you're dragging me off to see."

"I'm dragging you off to opportunity."

"Why drag me anywhere? Why not let me go when I feel ready?"

Kara backed off a step. She looked away. "I can't," she said.

"Why not?"

"Because."

"Because what?" I insisted. "Why do you even care what Ray does?"

She closed her eyes and took a breath. "If you could just see this guy."

"You sound as if you hate him."

Kara opened her eyes. "I know I'm not supposed to hate, Mark. I know it's wrong."

"Nobody's perfect."

"Vincent is," she said.

"Really?"

"Yes." She glanced at her watch, then at the setting sun. "But I'm not."

"Kara, why don't we—"

She came to a decision. She grabbed my arm again. "You're coming. Now. Don't say anything. Just watch and learn and thank me later."

I hoped Vincent took long showers. I gave in.

Kara drove a red Ferrari. She and Vincent must have purchased the cars at a two-for-one sale. She drove fast, fearlessly, and I thought each curve we went into would be our last. I realized I should never have told Kara where Ray worked. In fact, I couldn't even remember when I had told her. Maybe Becky had told her. I had been in to see Becky a number of times since I had met Kara and Vincent. Becky confirmed that she had spoken to Vincent about me, but she never mentioned Kara, and I hadn't brought her up.

It was after eight o'clock and just getting dark when we drove up to the mall where Ray worked. Kara jumped out of the car without locking it. One of these days, I thought, these two were going to get a rude awakening. I had quizzed Vincent once about where he got his money and had learned nothing more than it was in the family.

Kara had me enter the store first. She didn't want Ray to think we were together. That set off all kinds of alarms in my head. But I didn't argue with her. It wouldn't have done any good.

I had no trouble identifying Ray. My psychic powers were operating at peak performance. He had a name tag on. He was shelving books as I strolled past. He didn't ask if I needed help. I was disappointed to see that he was tall, strong, and handsome. It gave me a sinking feeling just watching him rip open the boxes of books with only his hands. He was not someone I wanted to annoy. He would have been soap-opera pretty if it hadn't been for his expression, which was very intense. On the other hand, he looked intelligent, like someone who was planning a future. He wore dress slacks and a tailored shirt—his family probably had money, too. His dark hair was cut short, almost a crew cut. Judging by his muscles, I decided he had probably played football in high school. Those days looked a couple years behind him now, though.

I walked by him without saying a word and hid behind the New Age section. I picked up a book on reincarnation and was halfway through the first page when Kara entered. I could see them both by rising up on my toes and peering over the astrology books. My major suspicion was immediately confirmed.

"Kara," Ray said, delighted. "I was just thinking of you."

"What?" Kara asked, laying on the charm. "You can think of me and work at the same time?"

Ray set aside his boxes and stood tall, puffing up his chest. "What brings you here?" he asked.

Kara let her eyes swim over the rows of books as if she was a dizzy blonde searching for one that didn't have too many words. "I'm looking for something inspirational," she said.

Ray pointed over his shoulder. "Our sex manuals are in the back."

Kara moistened her lips. "I already own enough of those."

Christ, I thought. It only got worse.

Ray grinned. "I bet you came by to see me."

Kara played with her hair. "Maybe. Maybe not."

"I know you did," he said. "Hey, I get off in an hour. You want to grab a bite to eat?"

"I can't. I'm busy."

"You told me that last time."

"What can I say? I'm a busy girl. I'm busy every day this week except tomorrow night."

Ray was encouraged. "I'm off tomorrow." Kara just gave him a blank stare. He added, "Do you want to get together?"

Kara thought for a moment. "What would your wife say?"

Ray laughed. He had undergone a personality transformation since Kara had appeared. He was full of fun now. "I'm not married. Whatever gave you that idea?"

Kara frowned. "You don't have a girlfriend?"

Ray didn't hesitate. "No."

Kara smiled with relief. "Where do you want to meet?"

"Why don't you give me your phone number?" Ray said.

"Because I don't want you talking to my boyfriend," Kara said and tapped him playfully on the chest. "I'll meet you here at six. I'll be hungry."

That was fine with Ray. Kara left the store moments later. I waited a few minutes before following. Ray gave me a curious stare as I walked by. Maybe he thought I was stealing a book.

Kara was sitting behind the wheel of her sports car, looking pleased with herself, when I caught up with her. Not saying a word, I climbed in and stared straight ahead.

"What's the matter?" she asked.

"Nothing," I said.

"I told you, Mark."

"I believed you when you told me. I didn't need a demonstration."

"He's no good. He's a liar and a cheat."

"He's a young man and you're a pretty girl and you threw yourself at him. You set him up."

"To prove a point. If you were going with Becky and I flirted with you like that, would you have asked me out?"

"No, I'm not Ray. But if I was Ray and I learned what you just did, I'd be angry."

Kara looked hurt. "You're mad at me."

I peered at her. She was still playing with her hair, but now she was tying it in knots. The strength of her reaction to my disapproval surprised me.

"No, I'm not," I said honestly. "I'm confused. I don't understand why you're going to all this trouble on my behalf."

"I want you to be happy."

"Why?"

"You're my friend," she said.

"Seeing you go out with Ray doesn't make me happy, Kara. What will Vincent say?"

"Nothing. He lets me do whatever I want."

"Are you really going to go out with Ray?"

"Yes."

"But you've made your point. He's a liar and a cheat. I told you I believe you." When she didn't answer immediately, I thought I understood why. "You're going to try to break them up, aren't you?"

"How could I possibly break up two people who are in love?"

I shook my head. "I won't have anything to do with this."

She turned and took my hand. "Listen, Mark, I said that sarcastically, but I meant it. I can't ruin their relationship if it's strong."

"That's not the point. None of this is your business. You're trying to decide things for them, for me, and you can't do that. You can't play God, Kara."

She let go of my hand and sat back. Together, without speaking, we watched as the last shoppers left the mall. The issue remained unresolved between us. It was dark now, and the parking lot was all but empty. Soon the employees inside would finish locking up, and the last of them would drive away. Kara must have been reading my mind.

She pointed toward a red BMW. "That's his car."

"How do you know?"

"I know."

"At least if you go to a drive-in, you'll be comfortable."

She smiled faintly. "I could bring one of my sex manuals."

I had to chuckle. "Really, Kara, that was crude."

"For someone who thinks she's God?"

"I didn't mean it that way."

"No," Kara said, staring at the BMW. "You weren't far off."

CHAPTER FOUR

At ten o'clock the next night I watched the earth die once more. But this time it was different. As I slid back from the keyboard, the Chinese didn't have a missile left to fire at me and my space station was still spinning, unharmed, with everyone on board alive. I hadn't realized how obsessed I'd become with the game. I let out a shout of triumph. Vincent wandered back into the room.

"I did it," I told him. "I survived."

He sat on the extra chair beside the computer. "How's China?"

"Smoking."

"How about the United States?" he asked.

"The same. The whole planet's fried. But I'm still here."

"Now what?" Vincent asked.

I shrugged. I had been hoping he'd at least congratulate me. Vincent had already become something of an idol to me. He was so cool. I was trying to earn his approval, I suppose, which made it difficult to criticize him.

"That's up to you," I said. "This isn't a satisfactory way to end. If even a portion of the U.S. could survive, there'd be hope the world could be rebuilt. Realism's fine, but despair is such a turnoff." I paused, squinting at the screen. "What's that?"

"Hope?" he asked and smiled.

As always, Vincent's graphics were superb—his world in ruin was particularly effective. The majority of radiation was, of course, invisible to the human eye, but Vincent had shown "hot" areas with pulsing waves of color. For example, New York City and Beijing, which inevitably suffered a dozen direct hits apiece, were throbbing with violet light on the globe below. But then, from seemingly nowhere, a number of barely defined glowing white balls began to cluster around the space station.

"What are those?" I asked.

"The next level of the game," Vincent said.

"Huh?"

"They are there to help you."

"I don't need any help. I'm safe."

"For the time being. But this space station isn't self-sustaining. You'll starve without regular supplies. You'll suffocate."

"Says who?"

"It's the way it is," Vincent said.

"What are these white balls? Are they aliens come to rescue me in their flying saucers?"

"They could be."

"You're going to have to do better than that," I said.

Vincent was not offended. "Tell me what you'd do."

I pointed to the screen. "First of all, if these are alien craft, you're going to have to picture them a lot more clearly. Frankly, I'm surprised. Visually, you're always top-notch. You know what these look like?"

"What?"

"Nothing," I said. "Balls of light."

"I didn't actually say they were flying saucers."

"That leads me to my second point. I don't care what they are. To suddenly have outside help at the end of the game is a cop-out. What are these white balls going to do, miraculously counteract all the radiation? You can't have divine intervention."

Vincent was interested. "Like angels?"

"Yeah. I mean, no. You don't want angels suddenly showing up and fixing everything that's wrong. You've got to win or lose with what you had to start the game."

Vincent nodded. "I agree."

"Then take these white balls out."

Vincent stared at the screen. So many of them had gathered about the space station that it had become hard to see. "But I like them," he said.

"Listen, this is a science-fiction game. You can't bring in supernatural creatures. You'll annoy the purists, and they're your biggest market."

"Then what if they are aliens?"

"Don't you know what they are?" I asked, getting exasperated.

"I'm asking what you would do with them."

"I've told you."

Vincent sat back and lowered his head. "Oh."

I turned off the screen. "It's getting late."

He looked up. "Don't you want to play anymore?"

I checked my watch. "It's after ten."

"So?"

I stood and stretched. Kara had told Vincent she was going out with Ray, and he had reacted exactly as she had predicted, by showing no reaction at all. She had left at five o'clock, although the mall was less than thirty minutes away. She said Ray was going to leave early.

"No, I don't want to play," I said and began to pace the floor. "Don't you care that your girlfriend's out with another guy?"

"Don't worry about Kara. She'll be all right."

"Aren't you jealous?"

"No."

"Why not?"

"I trust her."

He said it with such simple innocence that I felt guilty. But truthfully, I had no reason. I had never even entertained the thought of what it would be like to have Kara for a girlfriend, to take her away from Vincent. As he watched me pace, I couldn't rid myself of the feeling that he knew exactly what I was thinking. And for that reason, he trusted me, too.

"Don't worry, Mark," he repeated.

"But do you know what she's trying to do?"

"Yes."

"She's trying to break up Becky and her boy-friend."

"Yes."

I stopped. "Do you think that's right?"

"It's what she wants to do."

"You didn't answer my question," I said.

He smiled. "I tried."

"Vincent—"

"All we can do is try to do what we think is right," he went on, gazing out his bedroom window at the city lights below. "What happens from that point on is not up to us. It's like the computer program in this game. You can choose what course to take, but the consequences of that course are already set."

"Is that your personal philosophy of life?" I asked in a kidding tone. I had never seen him so serious before. But maybe he wasn't being serious now. He smiled again.

"It's the way it is," he said.

"But about Kara. I think she's making a mistake."

"Are you afraid of her mistakes, or are you afraid that you might try to profit from them and end up making your own mistakes?"

It was an insightful question. In fact, he had hit the nail right on the head. I didn't want Kara to succeed in breaking them up. If she did, and I went chasing after Becky and still didn't get her, then I would have no excuse. I would be unloved simply for who I was.

Ray was a safety net that protected me from reality. What I mean is, I often fantasized about being with Becky, but I never believed I would be, not really.

Vincent was peering at me in the same way he peered through his telescope—completely interested, yet also completely detached. My life to him was like some remote occurrence, worthy of respect, but nothing to cry over. I can't explain how such a perception of him didn't make him seem any less warm.

"I'm afraid of hurting Becky," I said finally.

"Yes?"

I hesitated. "And I'm afraid that what you said is true."

He nodded. "It's the game."

I was confused. "What does it have to do with your game?"

He wasn't given a chance to respond. Kara popped through the front door right then. I hurried into the living room to greet her, Vincent following at a substantially slower pace. Kara gave me a quick hug in greeting and then slipped into the kitchen. I had to go after her.

"How was your date?" I asked.

"We had fun, but he's a jerk."

"Are you going out with him again?" I asked.

She placed her purse on the bar, her head down. Her clothes were sexy—a short leather skirt, black high heels. I noticed her lipstick was smeared.

"I don't know if it's necessary," she said.

I felt relieved, for the moment. I didn't imagine that Kara could have made Ray forget the love of his life in one evening, even though she had almost done that to me.

"It's not necessary," I said, as Vincent came up beside me.

"Hi, honey," she said to him, raising her head only slightly.

"Hi," he said.

We stood that way for a long moment, Vincent and I together, Kara on the other side of the room. The two of us against her, or so it seemed. I assumed Vincent was on my side. Kara appeared to be deliberating over something. I could always tell when she was thinking. She would look sad.

"What is it?" I asked finally.

She spoke to the wall. "I saw a picture of Becky in his wallet."

"You looked in his wallet?" I asked.

"I did," she said.

"What for?" I asked.

"To see if he carried her picture," she said. "He was paying the bill at the restaurant. I just grabbed it out of his hand. I told him I wanted to see if he was really twenty years old. When I stumbled across Becky's picture, he told me she was his cousin."

"I might have done the same thing," I said.

Kara shook her head. "You wouldn't have lied to me."

"Lying isn't my style," I agreed. She heard the reproach in my voice. She continued to look away.

"I won't do this if you don't want me to," she said slowly. "But if you don't, Mark, you'll have to stop me. Otherwise, I'll do it."

"Do what?" I asked, glancing at Vincent, worried. Vincent looked as if we were discussing how many Chinese cities I had just destroyed while playing "Decision." He appeared as calm as ever. Kara finally glanced over at me. Her mascara was smeared, and I wondered if she'd been crying. Yet, when she spoke next, her voice was steady.

"I plan to go into Becky's store tomorrow," she said. "I'm going to have her help me find a record. Then I'm going to pretend to suddenly realize she's Ray's cousin." She nodded as my face darkened. "I'm going to tell her I was out with him the night before."

"I don't want you to do that," I said flatly, feeling hollow. My thoughts were not with Becky then, or how Kara's plan would ruin Becky's relationship with Ray. My mind was already grieving over the end of my friendship with Kara. For her even to conceive of such an act told me she could no longer be a friend of mine. It was ironic in a way. The whole magical mystery of my friendship with Kara had been the manner in which it had seemed to spring into being already firmly established. But I had only been fooling myself. What I was hearing told me I hadn't really known her at all.

"Before you decide," Kara said, "I want you to do me one favor."

"I've already decided," I said.

"I want you to visit Becky tonight," Kara went on. "She's still at the store. She's working late."

"How do you know?" I asked.

Kara held my eye. "I know."

"You're a jerk," I said bitterly.

Her lower lip trembled. She nodded. "But he's a bigger jerk."

"I'll warn Becky," I said.

"No, you won't," she said.

"I will!" I swore. "And don't tell me you know what I'll do!" I turned on Vincent. "Say something."

"Are we going out for ice cream?" he asked.

"Vincent," I pleaded. "What about Becky?"

"She can come if she wants," he said. Then he smiled to let me know he was no fool, or maybe a bigger fool than I could imagine for being with Kara in the first place.

I left the house, got in my car, and drove. I didn't know where I was going until I stopped the car and saw Becky through the window of her record store counting out a register. I just sat there, watching her without her knowing it. Then she turned off the store lights; she had been working alone. She stepped outside, and after she locked the door, she noticed me sitting in a car, watching her. But she didn't recognize me at first. She appeared to be frightened. Then suddenly she waved and hurried toward me.

"What are you doing here, you nut?" she asked, leaning into my open window.

"Thinking," I said.

"About your new game? I think I've almost cracked the 'Starlight Crystal.' My problem's been right in front of me all the time. I've figured out that the queen of the universe—'' She paused. "What's the matter, Mark?"

"Nothing."

"What are you doing here?" she asked.

"I came to see you."

"I wish you'd told me ahead of time. I can't stay and talk."

"Ray's waiting for you?"

Becky hesitated. She never brought up Ray unless I did. "I promised him yesterday that I'd stop by his place on my way home tonight."

"It figures," I said. It sure did. Becky had probably made the promise to Ray before he set his date with Kara. I'd been wrong to complain to Vincent that Ray and Kara were out late. Ten or ten-thirty was early to finish a date. But Ray knew he had to be home for Becky's visit. I had no illusions that Ray was going to tell Becky where he'd been. I felt I knew him well, and we hadn't even been formally introduced. Becky put her hand on my shoulder.

"I wish you had stopped by this afternoon," she said. "I was craving ice cream."

"You don't need me to eat it," I said, my melancholy refusing to depart. Becky surprised me. She leaned over and kissed my cheek.

"But with you it always tastes better," she said.

"When are you working next?"

"Tomorrow."

I coughed. "How about the time after that?"

"Monday night. Three to eleven. Are you going to come by?"

"Sure."

"You have to promise. I'll plan on it."

"I promise," I said.

"We could go to McDonald's together. Is six good for you?"

"It's good."

Becky sighed. "I wish you were coming by tomorrow. I hate Saturdays. They're so long."

"Yeah," I muttered, my guilt swelling in my lungs. "I know."

I could have suggested she stay home. I could have told her the whole story. I could have unleashed all my missiles on Beijing at once and concentrated my lasers on the Chinese submarines. Then maybe I would be a winner and there would be something left to show for it. Maybe Vincent had been right about it all being a game, right about his choice of titles— "Decision." It seemed the most important decisions I made were the ones where I decided to do nothing. Kara had me figured cold.

Yet that was all B.S. I didn't tell Becky that Kara was coming in to ruin her life because Becky suddenly leaned over and kissed me again on the cheek. That made twice in two minutes, and I couldn't remember when she had kissed me once. I loved it. I wanted a third, not necessarily right then, but Monday. Yes, I thought, Monday. Because of Kara, that was suddenly a possibility. An opportunity, as Kara had put it. Goddamn her. I wasn't just afraid of making a mistake. I was jumping at the opportunity.

"Good night, Mark," Becky said. "Take care of yourself."

"You, too."

"Monday?"

"I'll be here."

"Great," she said.

CHAPTER FIVE

Everything is inevitable once a decision has been made. Vincent said that and I believed him.

I didn't try to stop Kara. It was what she wanted to do. And even though I pretended to want to stop her, she was doing what I wanted, too. No wonder I felt so angry with her. I realize now that I only got angry when people did things that, deep inside, I knew I was capable of doing myself.

I didn't talk to either Vincent or Kara over the weekend. I waited until six the following Monday night before I visited Becky. As promised. What a hypocrite I was. On the drive to the record store, I kept hoping Becky had called in sick. But she was there, hard at work, even though she looked sick. One glance at her and I knew immediately that Kara had carried out her plan with cold-blooded efficiency.

"Hi," Becky said softly, glancing up from a box of

compact discs she was shelving. There were circles under her eyes.

"Hi," I said. "How are you doing?"

She went back to her job. "Fine."

I was brilliant, I must say. "What's new?" I asked.

"Nothing. How are you?"

"Great."

"That's good," she said.

I squatted beside her, my conscience crying out to tell her that it was all a setup. My vocal cords didn't hear a word of it. "Is something wrong?" I asked.

"No."

"Do you want to get something to eat?"

"No."

"Something to drink?"

She stopped working and stared at a CD cover for a moment. Her hands were trembling. "All right," she said.

She told the manager she was taking her break. We drove around the block to our usual ice-cream shop. We ordered Cokes and sat on a bench outside drinking them and watching the sky, not talking. The evening was warm and dry, but the sweat under my shirt was cold and sticky. I let Becky break the silence.

"I know I'm lousy company tonight," she said.

"That's OK."

"I had a bad weekend."

"Do you want to talk about it?"

She shook her head. "No."

"That's OK," I said.

"I broke up with Ray."

"You don't have to talk about it."

She sniffed. "I don't want to."

"That's OK."

"Thank you," she said, hanging her head. I put my hand on her back. If ever there was a time for an understatement. I couldn't believe what I said next.

"Don't thank me," I said. "I didn't do anything."

"Thanks for being my friend."

I forced a chuckle. "I'm not that great a friend."

She took my free hand and turned her damp eyes on me. "Yes, you are, Mark. When you come into the store, you always make me feel better. You make me laugh. I appreciate that. It means a lot to me."

"Well, I hope I never run out of jokes, then."

She smiled. "You're silly."

"A moment ago I was great."

"You are." She let go of my hand and took a sip of her drink, chewing on an ice cube, losing her smile. "He was such a jerk."

"Yeah."

"I should be happy."

"Yeah."

She set her drink down. "Do you want to go out?"

"Yeah. What? No. You just broke up. It wouldn't be right."

She snorted. She was angry. I had never seen her angry before. "Do you know what he did to me, Mark?"

"No."

"He went out with another girl. Friday night, when I was working late, he was out with another girl. Can you believe that?"

"You don't have to talk about it."

"I want to. He was out with this blond girl from Scotland. She came in my store the next day. She thought I was Ray's cousin. That's what he told her. Can you believe that?"

"Yeah."

"I hate him."

Becky was beginning to sound exactly the way Kara sounded when she talked about Ray. Minus the accent, of course, which Becky had so cleverly identified. It gave me a bad feeling.

"You shouldn't hate," I said.

She put her hands on her drink, but didn't pick it up. Her hands were trembling again. She swallowed the ice cube in her mouth.

"I know," she whispered.

She began to cry. I put an arm around her, and she sagged against my side, and I felt if she didn't stop soon I would tell her that Kara was *my* cousin. I would tell her anything to make the tears go away.

And I did. I told her the truth. Well, a big part of it. I told her I wanted to go out with her. It worked. She stopped crying. She asked me where we should go.

CHAPTER SIX

The following evening I was getting dressed for my date with Becky when someone knocked on the door of my tiny apartment. I seldom had visitors. The knock startled me. In the instant before I opened the door, a horrible thought flashed through my mind that it was Becky come to tell me she had changed her mind, that she was back with Ray. I had been looking forward to seeing her all day. I had barely slept the previous night. My resting pulse was in the low one hundreds, but I was feeling no pain.

Until the knock at the door. But then, it was only Kara, and I didn't know how to feel. She looked properly chastised—and beautiful.

"Can I come in?" she asked in a meek voice.

"I was just leaving."

"I know."

"Ah," I said. "What do you want?"

"To apologize."

"I'd think you'd be pleased at the turn of events. I'm surprised you're not here to tell me what to wear."

She inspected my clothes. "You know, you wear the same size as Vincent."

"Oh, Christ."

"You look good, Mark."

"You just implied that I looked awful."

"I mean your face." She stepped inside and took my hand. She pressed it to my chest and stared at me with her bright blue eyes. It was only then I noticed that she wore contacts. "You look happy," she said.

I shook my head. "You have some nerve."

"Are you still angry with me?"

"Yeah."

"Are you?" she asked again.

"No." I shook free of her and searched for my car keys. "I've got to get out of here."

Kara checked her watch. "You're picking her up at eight?"

"No, about nine."

"Where are you going now?"

"Don't you know? You know everything else."

"I hope you're going to get some decent clothes."

I put a hand to my head and closed my eyes. "I *was* going to buy some new clothes," I muttered.

"Why don't you wear some of Vincent's?"

I whirled around. "Is that why you're here? To tell me what to wear? What to say?"

"I know you'll think of something to say."

"Thanks."

"Are you sure you're not still angry with me?"

Suddenly I began to laugh. I didn't know why. Maybe because it felt good. It burst out of me. I laughed and laughed. Kara joined me. Crossing the room, she gave me a big hug.

"You'll have fun," she said, pressing her cheek to my face.

"I should have you shot," I said.

"Not tonight. Later. I have to hear every detail of your big date." She pulled away and slapped me on the rump. "Come on, we'll go in my car."

"So you're going to chauffeur us?"

"You're taking my car on your date. It's much more impressive."

"I doubt that Becky is so materialistic she'll be impressed by an expensive car."

"Don't think, Mark." Kara took my hand. "Let me do that for you."

Vincent wasn't home when we drove up. Kara thought he might be up at the cave setting up his telescope. Naturally, his absence didn't prevent her from plowing through his closet. Vincent had more clothes than I recalled from my last visit. Most of them looked as if they'd never been worn. I suspected that Kara had been out shopping that afternoon.

"You shouldn't wear blue," she said, pulling out a black leather coat. "You have dark hair, fair skin. You're definitely winter. You should throw away all your blue shirts. They look like your mother bought them for you."

"She did buy some of them." Several of the shirts

I owned went back to my freshman year in high school. Clothes had never been a priority with me.

"Well, you're not going out with your mother," Kara said, finding a pair of white pants and a red belt. I had never seen a red belt before, and I certainly couldn't see it around my waist. "You're going out with a woman. You've got to look sexy."

"It's almost eight," I said. "I don't have time to stop at a plastic surgeon on the way."

Kara was amused. "You're sexy, Mark. If it wasn't for Vincent, I would have seduced you weeks ago."

My heart did a nice natural skip that was infinitely preferable to the kind of thump caused by my defective valve. "Vincent might meet with an unfortunate accident on his walk back from the cave," I said hopefully.

She grinned and tossed me a handful of sex appeal. "Put these on."

"Wait in the other room."

"Of course," she said.

The clothes were just a bit loose; Vincent was more muscular than I was. Kara was pleased with the results, and I had to agree there was something to be said for the red belt after all, especially with the black leather boots Kara pushed on me next. I wondered if Becky would recognize me.

We walked up to the cave. We took it slow and easy. Kara let me stop and rest a number of times. I muttered something about being out of shape, and she just nodded her understanding. I felt a wave of intense love flow through me. And to think I had been furious with her only days before. I tried to figure it out but got nowhere.

Vincent had the telescope focused on the moon when we arrived. The sun had set, and the moon was about thirty degrees above the horizon, almost full. Kara was eager to look at it. Vincent didn't comment on my wearing his clothes. He seemed to be far away, serene as usual, yet preoccupied at the same time. He did ask about Becky, though.

"I'm going out with her tonight," I said.

He nodded. "You'll have fun."

"I hope *she* does," I said.

"Of course she will," Kara said, her eye pressed to the eyepiece. "Hey, Mark, you've got to see this. It's so big and bright."

Kara stepped aside and let me have a peek. I immediately reached for the focusing knob. Kara must have had sharper sight than I did. For a moment the moon was like one of those blurred balls of light in Vincent's game. The similarity struck me so strongly that for a moment I felt disoriented, as if I were seeing two moons at once. Then I noticed Vincent had his head pressed close to mine; he was fiddling with the smaller finder telescope strapped to the side of the main instrument. I thought my double vision must be a result of his shaking the telescope stand. Yet when I put my hand on the stand to steady it, the two moons didn't go away. My double vision actually intensified, and I had to step back from the eyepiece. I feared I was about to have a dizzy spell as I had the first night. But as quickly as it had come, it stopped.

"Are you all right?" Kara asked me.

I sucked in a deep breath. "I'm fine."

Vincent was also watching me. "Kara, why don't you show Mark the cave," he said.

"Yeah," I said. "I'd like to see this mysterious cave."

While Vincent stayed with the telescope, I followed Kara through the bushes to the opening of the cave. It was nothing spectacular, at least at first glance. The entrance was less than five feet high, so we had to stoop to enter. It was dark inside, naturally, but Kara carried a flashlight and flicked it on, revealing rough rock walls, an uneven dirt floor. The odor, however, struck me as unusual. The air inside the cave smelled fresh, like a forest after a spring shower.

"What do you do in here?" I asked.

"Talk."

"About what?" I asked.

Kara was walking in front of me, leading the way. She paused and glanced over her shoulder. "You'd be amazed," she said.

Not far into the cave, perhaps a hundred feet, it opened into an oval space approximately twenty feet across and with plenty of head room. This was not the end of the cave—it continued through a narrower opening on the far side of the room—but it was obviously where Vincent stored his telescope and talked to his girlfriend. The sides of the room were equipped with several natural rock ledges, perfect for sitting. The happy couple had placed a few blankets over these and set a small table and gas lantern nearby. As I stood and watched, Kara lit the lantern and turned off her flashlight. She gestured for me to sit on a ledge beside her.

"There's a draft in here," I said, pointing to the dark hole across from us. "Have you ever explored where that leads?"

"Not all the way."

"It would be interesting to find out," I said.

"Not now."

"You're right. I shouldn't even be here now. I'll be late."

"Becky will wait for you. She expects you to be late."

"I suppose she told you that?" I asked.

"Would you believe me if I said yes?"

"No."

Kara smiled. In the soft glow from the lantern, she seemed years younger, a child, free from all cares. Yet it was not only the light. Overall, she seemed greatly relieved. She met my gaze.

"What are you thinking?" she asked.

"If I tell you, will you tell me what you're thinking?"

"Maybe."

"I'm not thinking anything," I said. "I just feel happy."

"It's the same with me." She drew in a breath and took in the cave with her eyes. "Do you notice how quiet it is here?"

"Now that you mention it. I can hear my own heart beating."

Her face suddenly went blank. "So can I," she whispered.

"Kara?"

She smiled quickly. "Nothing. What are you going to do tonight?"

"You mean you're not going to tell me?"

Kara turned businesslike. "You have to eat first. Take her to a nice restaurant. It doesn't matter what kind: Italian, French, Japanese—Becky didn't strike me as being picky."

"Not like she is with the kind of car I drive. Has it occurred to you that she might have seen your car in the parking lot when you visited her at the record store?"

"I had to go there. You said you forgave me."

"I do," I said. "But what about the car?"

"I doubt if she saw it. But you can take Vincent's if it makes you more comfortable. Now, after dinner you can ask her what she wants to do. Leave that part up to her."

"I was thinking of taking her to a movie."

"You can't talk at the movies. You should talk to her. Besides, it will probably be too late for a movie."

"What if I bring her here and we talk?" I asked.

My suggestion seemed to startle Kara. "What?"

"I was just kidding. What's the matter?"

Kara relaxed. "There'll be plenty of time for that later."

"Time for what?"

"You know."

"What?"

Kara shrugged. "Seducing her."

I chuckled, embarrassed. I hadn't known that was what she meant. "Are you sure?" I asked. "It seems I missed my chance with you when you met Vincent."

"That was a long time ago."

"Really? How long have you known him?"

"Many years."

"When did you meet?"

Kara checked her watch and stood up abruptly. "You'd better go."

I stood and stretched. "But you just said she would wait for me."

She took me by the hand and pulled me toward the entrance. "Sometimes I'm wrong," she said.

CHAPTER SEVEN

I ended up being exactly on time. Becky wasn't even ready. She had no sooner answered the door than she dashed back into her bedroom. I didn't know why; she looked great to me. I was left all alone in her deserted living room. Her parents had gone out for dinner. I hoped we wouldn't end up at the same restaurant. I had a sneaking suspicion they wouldn't approve of me after the smooth-talking Mr. Ray.

It was while I waited for Becky that I started to doubt my date was really going to happen. I guess at heart I was a pessimist, a dreamer. I knew I was bound to wake up any second and everything would vanish. I'm not kidding, walking around the living room, I actually pinched myself to see if I was where I thought I was. Yet there was something other than my date with Becky that filled me with a sense of unreality. Something about the two moons I'd seen up on the hill. Despite my dizziness and their blurred shapes, they had both seemed so vivid and real.

"Hi," Becky said finally, coming up behind me and taking me by surprise. "How do I look?"

Her taste in clothes was vastly different from Kara's, much more conservative. She wore a simple summer dress, white and cool, covered with green flowers and singing birds. With her warm smile and her sweet welcome hug, I counted our date a success already. I hadn't wanted to spend the night mourning for Ray with her.

"You look like the queen of the universe," I said.

She laughed. "You know, when we come back here tonight you're going to help me crack that stupid game of yours."

"No way. Then you won't need me anymore."

She took me by the arm and led me toward the door. I was reminded of Kara leading me out of the cave. "I'll always need you to help me with something," she said.

We went outside to my car—to my black Ferrari. Kara had been right. Becky was impressed. She muttered something about the royalties I must be getting. I muttered something back about its being stolen.

We headed down to the beach. It was a crazy idea—the beach was twenty miles away. On the drive there, our conversation flowed easily. We talked about nothing of importance, the kind of talks I find are usually the most important. We even discussed the weather. It was hot. It had been hot all summer. But soon summer would be over. I kept glancing at the moon as we drove. Almost full, I thought. The love of my life was finally sitting beside me, but I couldn't keep my eyes off the moon. A sense of loss plagued me. It was the sight of the moon that brought the haunted feeling, but I didn't know why.

Yet I was happy. Vague forebodings can't compete with a real live girl. Becky was in good spirits. She cracked one joke after another, half of them at my expense. I didn't mind. We drove with the windows down, the wind in our hair.

I chose the restaurant. Becky put up a bit of a fuss—she thought it was too expensive. It overlooked the water, and the clientele coming out the front door carried gold toothpicks. Because I was driving a Ferrari, I told her, we couldn't very well go to McDonald's.

The meal was a new experience for me. We had three waiters attending us, and my cup of coffee was never allowed to slip below the halfway point. Becky ate lightly, a salad for a bunny, but I managed to choke down a thick steak. A man's meal, as they say. We left the restaurant with me totally stuffed.

Then the fun started, but it was not good clean fun. It was a nightmare.

Walking to the car, we spotted a couple of oil wells a little way down the beach by the water. We were in a classy neighborhood, but in southern California by the beaches, oil wells are not out of place. These two were cranking full speed, up and down. I innocently remarked how as a child I used to climb oil wells and ride them. Becky was instantly intrigued.

"Could we do that?" she asked.

"You mean now?"

"Yeah. It looks like fun."

"No," I said. "You'd get your dress all dirty."

"I don't care. I want to do it."

"There's a fence around each well."

"We'll climb it." She gave me a sly grin. "Scared?"

That got me. I'm sure it was a male ego thing. With my poor heart and all, I'd always been particularly sensitive about being regarded as a wimp. I figured we could climb the fence, and once Becky saw how big the wells were up close, she'd back off. I didn't stop to think how weird it was that she wanted to ride one of the oily monsters in the first place.

It was a short drive to the wells. Becky bounded out of the car and across the sand before I could put on the Ferrari's parking brake. She attacked the fence surrounding the wells. Kicking off her shoes, she was over it in a few seconds. I took a lot longer with my climb, even though she implored me to hurry. I figured having a heart attack would only spoil the evening.

The wells were remarkably quiet. They must have been of a recent design, although they were both coated with rust. The ocean air was to blame for that. They towered above us like hungry insects plowing the earth for fresh meat. A metal ladder led up each side. As kids we used to climb similar ladders and then crawl onto the head of the arm of the well. But even as a kid, I never climbed such a huge well.

"This is crazy," I said.

Becky put a foot on the ladder. "It'll be exciting."

"Why do you want to do this?"

"Why not? Are you coming, Mark?"

"I'll mess up my clothes." Or Vincent's clothes, I thought. Not that he'd care, probably.

"Come on," she insisted.

I followed her up the ladder. She had on pink underwear. I couldn't help but notice. The moon shone brilliantly across the beach. I half hoped a policeman would swing by and give us a strict scolding. As I looked down from near the top of the ladder, a wave of anxiety and dizziness swept over me and I had to grip the metal bar tightly.

"What do we do next?" she asked.

"Say a prayer. We should get down."

"How do you climb onto this thing?" Becky asked, gesturing to the rising and falling arm. I called it an arm, but as it swooped rhythmically by, driving its pipe deeper and deeper into the earth, it looked more like an angry fist.

"Carefully," I answered.

"Tell me."

"That's how you do it. You just catch it and climb on. But I warn you, if you panic and want to stop, it won't stop. We can't stop it."

She ignored me. She climbed onto the arm, initially pulling herself up with her arms, before throwing her legs over the top of the metal. I took the ladder up another few rungs. Becky was having a great time. Hugging the blasted thing with both arms, rocking up and down, she smiled over at me.

"This isn't so bad," she said.

"Just stay where you are. If you climb out toward the end, you'll feel like you're riding a tornado."

I'm a master of suggestion. Becky did exactly what I didn't want her to do, and then some. She crept *all* the way to the end, until she was straddling the arm just above the huge insectlike head. Her hair flew up in the night, and she threw back her head and laughed.

"I love it!" she said. "Come on, Mark."

"No."

"You've got to try it."

"Becky, please get down."

"I'm fine. Don't worry."

"You're going to get dizzy," I said.

Another suggestion. I didn't mean it that way. I meant it as a warning. But suddenly, as Becky stared up at the moon, the dizziness hit her. She began to panic. I knew exactly how she felt. I had warned her. That sudden overwhelming desire to have the world stand still. It hit her with irrational speed and didn't respond well to logic. Even though nothing had changed for her in the last few seconds, I knew she was now afraid she was going to die. She threw herself onto the metal arm, hugging it with both her arms and legs.

"Mark!" she cried. "I'm going to throw up."

"Hang on. You'll be fine."

"I'm going to fall, Mark. Help me!"

I responded too hastily to her panic. I should have tried to talk her down. By going to her rescue, I blocked her way back to the ladder. But I did it anyway. I had just eaten steak. I was a man. I had to save my woman.

I had little trouble climbing onto the arm of the well. Despite my lack of strength and endurance, I'm extremely well coordinated. But I had a full stomach, and the rocking motion quickly let me know it. Creeping toward the head of the arm, with the strength of the ride growing in intensity as I edged forward, I also began to feel as though I would vomit. Yet none of my fear for myself matched my fear of Becky's fear. Her leg grip was weakening. Her hips had begun to rock to the side. I glanced straight down into a mess of gears and motors. If she fell, she wouldn't have a soft landing.

"Mark!" she screamed.

"I'm coming. Keep your eyes open. Stare at the road, anything stationary. You're going to be fine."

I reached her in a matter of seconds. Now my problems really began. It was not as though I could ease her onto my shoulders and carry her safely back to civilization. Indeed, I couldn't budge her an inch. Her legs might have been losing their strength, but her hands were dug so tightly into the rusty lip of the oil well arm that her fingers were bleeding. She cried pitifully.

"I have to get down," she said. "Please help me down."

"You're going to have to let yourself slide backward. It's easy. Each time we swing upward, loosen your grip slightly. Tighten it as we swing down." Naturally, she sat with her back toward me; she had crept headfirst toward the end of the arm. I leaned forward and wrapped my arm around her waist, an arm I could ill afford to spare at the moment. I spoke in her ear. "Trust me, Becky. I will not let you fall."

She nodded her head weakly. She loosened her

vise grip when we were going up. Slowly, painfully, we inched back toward the ladder, the center of balance, where the waves were kinder. It didn't take us long to reach our goal, although it seemed like forever. Once there, we had to deal with the next big obstacle to freedom and safety from the metal monster: I was still in her way. I had to climb off. I had to let go of her. But she wouldn't let me.

"I can't hold on," she gasped. "I'll fall off."

"I'll just have to let go of you for a second."

"No!"

I had no choice. She could cry all she wanted. In her condition, I knew there was no way she'd be able to climb onto the ladder without my assistance. Backing up farther, past the ladder, was therefore out of the question on my part.

"Just hang on," I said.

"No! Mark, no!"

I let go of her and swung onto the ladder in one smooth motion. It turned out to be easier than I thought. Unfortunately, Becky's dizziness had worsened. She didn't know what was up and what was down, and never mind that she was now close to the center of balance and was no longer rocketing into the sky every few seconds. I couldn't get her to swing her legs down onto the rungs of the ladder. I couldn't even get her to respond to my voice. She had buried her head in the metal arm. She was crying. I was afraid she'd go into shock next.

Just then I noticed a metal pole lying on the ground near the base of the oil well. The pole was attached to a fallen sign that carried a wise warning that this was a hazardous area. I left Becky and climbed down the ladder in a moment. I picked up the pole, dragging the sign on the ground. The gears of the oil well motor were sheltered from rain but were wide open to any determined vandal.

"Hang on tight, Becky!" I called. "I'm going to stop this thing!"

Becky stirred. She raised her head and glanced down. She didn't speak, but only retightened her grip. I shoved the end of the pole into the motor.

Instantly it was snapped from my hands. I was lucky the sign didn't behead me. It flew into the gears with the rest of the pole. Something cold whisked by the tip of my ear. An awful noise followed. It sounded like—well, a pissed-off oil well. A screech rent the air. Orange sparks shot out at my feet. The arm of the well crawled slowly upward and got stuck. And for that I was thankful—that the oil well hadn't jerked to a halt and tossed Becky off. The noise stopped, and the silence that followed was like a blessing from above. I leapt back onto the ladder, trying to ignore my labored breathing and the growing pain in my chest.

Helping Becky down to the ground proved simple. I knew exactly how she must have felt when the oil well stopped moving. Infinite relief. Yeah, I'd got trapped on an oil well once when I was only eleven. I had been alone. When I had finally got down, I felt as if I'd aged eighty years.

We sat without talking for a few minutes, trying to catch our breath. Naturally, I took forever to recover. The pain in my chest receded in tiny gulps. Becky stood and stumbled to the fence that surrounded the wells and leaned against it. She didn't have to reclimb it. For the first time I noticed a hole in the sand beneath the fence. I pointed it out to her, and she nodded without a word and used it to slip under the fence. She didn't have to worry about her dress now. She was a mess. I followed her shortly, feeling limp and spent. Becky wandered down to the water. Close to the edge of the waves, she plopped down in the sand, her head buried in her knees. I sat beside her. She had stopped crying, and I took that as a sign of progress. Until she spoke.

"He's probably out with her now," she said.

Of course I knew who the *he* and *she* were. I realized in an instant what was going on. Ever since I had picked her up, Becky had been unusually jovial, almost wired. She was trying to block it all out. I made a good block. So did risking her life. She really cared about Ray. The whole situation made me feel awful.

"I bet he's not," I said.

"How would you know?"

"I don't know."

She glanced up. Her face was dry. "I'm sorry. I shouldn't have said that."

"It's all right. How do you feel?"

Disgust wrinkled her features. "Like an idiot."

"It's good to feel that way every now and then. It keeps us humble."

"Have you ever felt this way?" she asked.

"Yeah."

"When?"

"When I first asked you out and you said no."

"I'm sorry," she said.

"Don't be. The feeling went away when you said yes."

She shook her head helplessly. "It hit me so suddenly. I felt so dizzy. I thought I was going to die."

"I know the feeling." I paused. "Do you miss him?"

She looked out over the ocean. She nodded. "Yeah."

"Do you want to go home?"

She continued to stare at the water, the waves. They were small but well formed, sleek curves of moonlit glass.

"Mark," she said, "what's the big secret in your game?"

"Your traveling companion on your quest is your worst enemy."

She frowned. "But you choose a different companion each time."

"It doesn't matter. They're always against you. You have to kill them at the first opportunity. Then you can make rapid progress."

"Why did you make it that way?"

I shrugged. "I wanted it to be unique."

"That doesn't seem like much of a reason. Is Chaneen, the queen of the universe, an enemy, too?"

"She's the only exception. But that's all I'll tell you. What's your first name?"

Her face changed, but I wasn't sure how. She appeared to go still, to turn inward. Without moving her head, she let her eyes stray to the moon above. My own eyes did the same, and for a moment I had the sudden conviction that Vincent was still on his hill with his telescope, looking at the moon. The conviction carried with it a peculiar sense of déjà vu.

"I don't want to go home," she said softly.

"You're changing the subject."

She looked directly at me. "I want to go to your place."

"Why?"

"Don't ask why."

"But—" I wanted to say something about Ray without speaking his name. I wanted to tell her she had to get over him before she could get to know me. She didn't give me the chance. She leaned over and kissed me on the lips.

"You risked your life to save me," she whispered into my ear as she held her cheek to mine. "Can you tell me why?"

She didn't know that I could but wouldn't. Regrettably, my love for her was not the only answer. I was no better than my computer-generated characters. Because of me, Becky had gone up on the oil well in the first place. Because of Kara and me, she had broken up with Ray. I was her worst enemy. But I said nothing. I stood and brushed off my pants and led her back to the car.

We passed the wrecked oil well as we drove back to the main road. Someday, I thought, when I was rich, I would send the oil company a check.

* * *

Becky stayed late at my place, although not the entire night. We didn't talk much. We didn't have sex. We just lay beside each other on my bed and rested, listening to each other's heartbeats. Once during the night she pressed her hand to my chest and asked if I was all right. She must have noticed the irregularity in the beat. I told her I was fine. Then I thought of Kara, probably waiting up late to hear how the date had gone, and I smiled. I would tell her the same thing. It went fine, just fine.

CHAPTER EIGHT

The next morning Kara came early and knocked softly on my door. I knew who it was without asking. I shouted for her to come in. She peeked through a crack in the door before opening it all the way.

"Just wanted to be sure you were alone," she said.

Kara had on torn blue jeans and a black T-shirt. She plopped down on the bed beside me. I had only a white sheet and my underwear for covering. That was all. Yet I didn't feel uncomfortable. Kara kissed me on the forehead, her blond curls falling all over my pillow.

"We didn't see you last night," she said.

"Tell Vincent I'm sorry I didn't bring the car back."

"Vincent says you can keep the car."

"Right," I said.

"Really. You can stay at our house. We're going away on an extended vacation."

I sat up with a start. "Where are you going?"

Kara sat up slowly. "Far away."

"Where? For how long?"

Kara spoke gently. "I can't tell you where we're going. It's a secret. But we'll be gone a long time."

"Why can't you tell me?"

"I just can't tell you." She touched my hand. "You have to trust me on this and accept my answer. It's what Vincent wants, too."

"But I haven't had a chance to help him with his game. All I've done is play it. You two can't leave now."

Kara smiled a sad smile. I know she didn't intend it, but I suddenly felt as if I were her child, a child about to lose his mother.

"You helped him more than you know," she said. "He wanted me to tell you that."

"I'm not going to get to say good-bye to him?"

"I'm afraid not." She leaned over and kissed me again, this time on the lips. "Don't worry, Mark. Everything will be all right."

I had never cried in front of a girl, or in front of anyone, for that matter—at least not since I was a little kid. I didn't cry then. But I came so close to weeping that my eyes stung and I had to cover them with my hand.

"You can't go," I said, and there was so much wrapped up in those three small words it would have taken volumes to explain. But I think Kara heard and understood it all. Kara and Vincent's appearance in my life had been like a moon rising on a dark night. I couldn't bear the thought of going back to being by myself. Kara seemed to read my mind, as she so often did.

"You have Becky now," she said. "You don't need Vincent and me."

I stood and walked to the sink and drank a glass of water. I stared out the window, not caring about Kara's seeing my underwear. The sky was blue overhead, but there were clouds on the horizon. Maybe there would be a storm later that night, I thought, to cover up the moon. It was then I remembered my premonition of loss and recognized how accurate it had been.

"I don't have Becky," I said.

"Yes, you do."

"You haven't even asked how our date went."

"I know it went well."

"What would you say if I told you she almost died?"

Kara hesitated. "Really?"

"Yes."

"Then I would say it was probably you who saved her from dying."

I bit my lip softly, not enough to draw blood but hard enough to feel pain. That was the thing about physical pain. It was real. It was simple to understand, unlike other kinds of pain.

"I don't understand any of this," I said. "You come here out of nowhere, set me up with Becky, and then disappear back into nowhere. Were Becky and I your reason for coming?"

"Our reasons were complicated," Kara said.

"Will you ever come back? A simple uncomplicated yes or no would be appreciated."

"No."

I put down my glass of water. Actually, I dropped it. The glass shattered. Then my finger was bleeding. I didn't feel the cut—it was too sharp, too sudden. Kara stood and wrapped my bloody finger in a white paper towel that quickly turned red.

"Are you all right?" she asked.

"Yes."

"Did you have fun last night?"

"Yes."

She nodded. "I'm glad."

"I promised I'd call Becky when I woke up."

"You're awake now." Kara gestured to the phone. "Go ahead, let me listen. I fought for this, you know."

I dialed the number. I didn't know why I didn't wait. Maybe I was trying to keep Kara there longer. I felt as if she would leave any second and just be gone forever. I got blood all over Becky's numbers. She answered on the third ring.

"Hello, Becky? It's me, Mark."

She hung up the phone.

"What's wrong?" Kara asked, standing near the kitchen sink. I stared at the dial tone sounding in the receiver. Yeah, stared at it. Then I slowly put the phone down.

"I don't know," I said.

Kara sat down beside me on the bed. "Dial her again."

"She hung up on me," I said.

"You might have had the wrong number."

"It was Becky," I said.

"Maybe she got disconnected. Try her again."

This time I punched out the number with my uninjured hand. It rang and rang—ten times. A big ten times.

"Maybe she's not home," Kara said.

"She was home a second ago." I set down the phone again. "She hung up on me."

Kara was concerned. "There must be some mistake. Try it again."

"No."

"Are you sure you dialed the right number?"

Becky had given me her number when we arranged our date. I had instantly memorized it, but now I studied the wrinkled slip of paper on the wooden stand beside my bed.

"Nine-four-three," I said, "eight-one-two-two."

Kara frowned. "That's right."

"How do you know her number?"

"Never mind. Today's Wednesday. She starts work at ten. She'll be going in soon. You have to talk to her."

"She doesn't want to talk to me."

Kara stood and began to pace. "Don't you want to know why?"

I swallowed thickly. It was turning out to be one lousy day, and I only had my underwear on. "I don't know."

Kara grew impatient. "We have to find out what's going on before I leave. I have to know."

"Maybe she went back to Ray."

Kara whirled on me. "Don't say that! Don't even joke about that!"

"I wasn't joking."

Kara grabbed my pants and threw them at me. "Get dressed. We're going to the record store."

CHAPTER NINE

Kara drove. She drove as only she knew how—fast and dangerously. I tried to pass the time by not thinking. It was amazing how difficult it was. Time was my enemy now, I thought. But then, when was it ever a friend to anybody? It killed us all. My heart ached. I felt as if I was dying inside.

Kara parked around the block from the record store. "Talk to her," she said.

"It isn't ten yet."

"She always goes in a few minutes early."

"Why do I have to ask her why she hung up on me? Why don't you just tell me? You tell me everything else about her."

Kara closed her eyes and sighed. "Because I don't know, Mark."

I got out of the car. I can't say the walk to the record store did me good. I was feeling more than sorry for myself.

Kara was right. Becky had come in early. She stood behind the cash register, exactly as she had when we first met. But she took one look at me and immediately strode into the back where only employees were allowed. I followed her. I mean, I wasn't worried about getting fired. Fortunately the storage area was deserted.

"Becky," I said, "what's wrong?"

She stood with her back toward me, reeking of disdain for the woman who had borne me. "Why don't you ask your girlfriend?" she said, so quietly I could hardly hear her.

"I don't have a girlfriend."

"Ray says you do."

"She's not my girlfriend."

"Is she your cousin?" she asked.

"Becky, I can explain."

She turned on me and pointed toward the emergency door. It was one of those kinds with an attached alarm.

"Get the hell out of here!" she screamed.

I recoiled at the words. I had never heard Becky cuss before. "Could I first tell you my side of the story?" I asked.

Her anger had enlarged her eyes, and I felt so small in them. "Your *story*," she said bitterly. "This is not one of your stupid games. I loved Ray. He was my boyfriend. We were happy together. And then you came along and set him up with that girl, who set me up . . ."

Becky didn't finish. Her head dropped to her chest, and tears slipped down her face onto her shirt. She appeared to be as ashamed as she was angry, ashamed that she could have been stupid enough to fall for my scheme. I wanted to tell her it wasn't my scheme, but I didn't think she'd be stupid enough to believe my story, even though it was the truth. I decided it would be best if I just left. I could go buy a bottle of sleeping pills or a good strong rope, I thought. I stepped to the emergency exit and put my hand on the bright red bar. But before I could leave, I had to turn and say something. It seemed required.

"I had a great time last night," I said.

Becky nodded. "So did I."

"Goodbye," I said. She chose not to answer. I went through the door and into the sunlight. An alarm went off at my back. I kept walking. I considered walking all the way home, and to hell with Kara. But it would have taken me ten hours to get there, and I was already exhausted. I returned to Kara's red Ferrari. She was pacing in front of the car. A squad car swept by on the adjoining street, no doubt on its way to the record store.

"How did it go?" Kara asked.

"She knows."

"She knows what?" Kara demanded.

"What you did. That I was behind it."

"That's impossible."

"Yeah," I said.

"But you weren't behind it. I was."

"I suppose you could explain that to her right now," I said. "But considering that I just left, it might look kind of suspicious."

Kara slapped the hood of her car hard. "Dammit! There's no way she could have known."

"Ray told her," I said.

Kara jumped at that. "How could Ray have known?"

"I don't know." I opened the door on the passenger side. "Please drive me home. I don't feel so good."

Kara slammed the door shut before I could get in. She was shook, and it showed.

"We have to find out what happened," she said. "Don't you see, Mark? I have to know before I can leave."

"Why don't you just leave and not worry about my love life? I'll send you a postcard that explains it all."

Kara's expression was pinched with pain. "You blame me."

I sighed. "No," I said honestly. "I blame myself. I blame God. He has a weird sense of humor."

"God," Kara muttered to herself. She stared in the direction of the store. It was a long stare. Her breath was ragged and her lips were trembling, and then she wasn't breathing at all and her lips were white and bloodless. "Ray," she whispered.

"I doubt he'll want to go out with you again," I said.

Kara broke out of her trance and grabbed my hands. There was real fear in her eyes now. "We have to go see him," she said.

"No, I don't think so. I think I should go back to bed."

Kara let go of my hands and hurried around to the driver's side. She hadn't heard me. "Get in," she said. "He'll be at the bookstore. We'll go there. He can tell me what happened."

"He might just kill you," I warned, opening the car door.

Kara didn't hear that, either.

We spent the drive to the mall listening to the radio. Every station was playing commercials. I felt so flat that I wondered if the music didn't just sound like commercials. My depression was so deep that there was no room for anger or blame. I tried to tell Kara it was all right, that she should just go off with Vincent and be happy on Saturn or Jupiter or wherever she was going. I tried to reach over and give her a reassuring pat on the leg. My hand bumped into the stick. She was shifting into fifth, running a red light at ninety miles an hour. If she was trying to kill us, I decided not to complain.

By the time we reached the mall, I had decided I'd better accompany her inside. She wasn't in favor of the idea.

"Are you crazy?" she asked.

"You're in no position to ask such a question," I said. "Why are we here? To ask Ray how he found out what you were up to? I warned you about that before. You met him at the mall for your date. You were driving a Ferrari. I drove a Ferrari when I went out with Becky. Who cares if it was a different color? It's a very unusual car for someone our age to have. If they talked, it could easily have come up. Then they could have become suspicious."

Kara shook her head. "She wouldn't have talked to him after she found out he was cheating on her."

"How do you know?"

"I know her."

"How?"

"Don't ask."

"But what if he called her?" I asked.

"Impossible. What happened to you this morning when you called?" Kara opened the door on her side. "Stay here. I'll be back in a few minutes."

"No." I stared at her. "No."

"You're the one he'll try to kill, Mark. There's more here than meets the eye. I have to talk to him alone."

"Then you can talk to him after I do."

Kara gave in. We went into the bookstore together. A young girl at the cash register told us Ray was working in the back. I tried to think of a nice way to introduce myself. Kara held my hand as we walked to the rear of the store. I shook her off. I wanted both hands free.

It didn't do me a bit of good.

We knocked on the door. Ray answered. He peered at us for a moment. Then his handsome face twisted into something that wasn't so handsome, and I caught a blur of fist out of the corner of my left eye. He was quick. I didn't even have a chance to raise my arm to block the punch. It caught me square on the nose. I dropped to my knees, blood spurting over my white T-shirt. I had worn the same shirt while I had lain in bed the night before with Becky. My vision went as red as my blood, but the fight had already been knocked out of me. He was a strong son of a bitch.

Kara came to my rescue, which I thought fitting. She jumped at Ray and shoved him back into boxes of books. She was trying to calm him down, but she might have used too much force. He shoved her away with one of his powerful arms, and she landed on her butt. A pity. Ray now had the chance to punch me again. He came after me and all I could do was watch.

"Ray," Kara cried, "it's not him."

Ray hesitated. I prayed the blood on my face had made me unrecognizable and that he had a short memory. Then it struck me that he must have had an incredible memory to associate me with the night he had asked Kara out. It didn't make sense that he knew automatically that I was the one who had been out with Becky, unless she had described me to him, which seemed unlikely. Kara got to her feet.

"Leave him alone," she told Ray. "We just want to talk to you."

"This isn't the guy who tried to steal my girlfriend?" Ray demanded.

"Your girlfriend?" Kara said. "You told me you didn't have a girlfriend."

Ray was not ashamed. "You didn't tell me you had a scheming partner."

"I'm not a scheming partner," I mumbled.

"Who the hell are you?" Ray turned and asked me.

"A friend of Becky's," I said. I have lousy timing, I really do. Ray drew back his fist and stepped forward. Kara grabbed hold of his arm and rode it several feet in the air.

"You have to listen to us, you idiot!" she yelled.

Ray stopped to listen. Even with an open vein inside my nose pumping out my life's blood, I couldn't help but be fascinated by the way Ray and Kara related to each other, like an old couple who were fed up with each other. Obviously, though, I wasn't nearly as perceptive as Ray. He turned toward Kara and his jaw dropped open.

"What happened to your accent?" he asked.

"That's right," I said. Kara was no longer the sweet Scottish lass. Indeed, she now sounded exactly like someone who had been born and raised in southern California. Kara stared at each of us before answering. It wasn't much of an answer.

"Never mind" was all she said.

"Who the hell are you?" Ray demanded of her.

"Yeah," I seconded. Kara was not intimidated.

"Who the hell told you about me?" she asked Ray.

"Why should I tell you?" Ray said.

Kara sucked in a hissing breath, and it was filled with cold vapors. But it was not directed at Ray. She had turned away to face the wall. Ray glanced at me and I shook my head. Suddenly he and I were in this together. Neither of us could see Kara's face.

"He was here," she whispered.

"Who was here?" I asked.

"Are you talking about Frederick?" Ray asked. "You know him? I guess you do. Yeah, he told me about you two slimes."

"When?" Kara asked.

"Last night," Ray said. "He came in the store. He's my kind of guy. He got right to the point about you two, didn't mess around." Ray threw me a wicked look. "He told me to watch out for you."

I raised my hands in a gesture of submission and got up slowly. Ray watched me the whole way. Obviously, this Frederick didn't have a high opinion of me. Ray put his hand on his sport coat pocket, and it made me wonder just how bad the opinion had been. Yet at the moment Kara was more my concern. She had been upset before, but now she was trembling.

"Let's get out of here," I told her, gently touching my nose and coming away with a handful of blood. "Come on, Kara."

Kara slowly turned back to Ray. She moved toward him as if in a dream—the information about Frederick's visit had obviously shocked her. She took a deep breath, as if to steady herself.

"If Frederick comes back," she said to Ray, her accent apparently gone for good, "be careful. He's dangerous, more dangerous than you can imagine."

Ray snorted. "You can't tell me anything, bitch. I just met him but at least I know he's honest."

Kara nodded faintly. "As honest as a loaded gun."

Again Ray's hand strayed to his coat pocket. He stopped himself when he realized what he was doing. Kara smiled thinly at him and shook her head; then she crossed the room. She took my hand and we left the store—out the back way, through another emergency exit, setting off another alarm.

Once outside, Kara didn't stop to look at my nose or comment on the loss of her Scottish accent. She ran for the pay phones located outside the mall entrance. I followed her as best I could, using the hem of my T-shirt for a handkerchief. But it's no easy task trying to chase after someone while keeping your head tilted back. By the time I caught up with her, she had already made her call and given up on getting an answer. She slammed down the receiver as I staggered to her side.

"Vincent's not home," she said.

"So?" I asked.

"He should be home. There's no reason for him to be out."

"Maybe he went to the store," I suggested.

She was upset. "Vincent doesn't go to stores!"

"Never?"

She grabbed my hand. It seemed she was always doing that, dragging me places I did not want to go. "Hurry," she said. "We have to go home."

"But I want to go back to bed."

"Mark!" she cried. "Vincent could be in trouble."

I stopped. "Is this Frederick really that bad?"

Her face seemed to fall all the way to her shaking knees. "Worse."

We hurried to the car. On the way to her house, I tried to find out about Frederick and about Kara's new nationality, but I got nowhere. I tried not to bleed on the Ferrari's upholstery. I wasn't really worried about Vincent, although I suppose I should have been. I wondered if Ray had, in fact, been carrying a gun in his jacket.

The door to the house was wide open. Kara barely stopped the car before jumping out and flying toward the porch. By now I had recovered somewhat. I caught up with her before she could enter.

"Me first," I said firmly, a hand on her arm. "No arguments."

Kara agreed. Leaving her on the porch, I stepped through the front door and into silence. Everything appeared to be normal, but nothing *felt* normal. The house rang with the hollow vibration that coffins must suffer after a visit from graverobbers. Yes, even before I saw it, the house reminded me of a coffin. An empty box that only sorrow could fill.

"Vincent?" I called.

I found it in the kitchen. It was all that I could do not to vomit. I was already covered with my own blood, but this blood touched me deeper, deep in that part where our mortality lives. For the second time in less than an hour I dropped to my knees. I would have prayed for another blow to my face to take the place of the pain I suffered in that moment, if only I believed the prayer would be answered.

The blood was all over the countertop, dripping drop by slow drop onto the floor. Right away I knew the surprise had been left there for me, as much as for Kara. It was obvious. Frederick's wicked stab was too personal to be understood in any other light. He must have known all about me, too. And what he knew must not have pleased him.

Sitting on the white-tiled countertop was a human heart—impaled on a shiny steel knife.

CHAPTER TEN

When the smoke finally cleared and Kara and I could think again and look with eyes that wouldn't close at the bloody sight, we decided the heart had not belonged to Vincent. It was old—it smelled of formaldehyde. It could have been stolen from a medical-school supply room, or even possibly swiped out of a high school biology class. But the blood was fresh, and God knew where Frederick had obtained it, although it was probably from an animal. It didn't have the consistency of human blood, and I had a fair amount of the latter available on my shirt with which to make a comparison.

Kara went to search for Vincent in the cave even though she knew it was hopeless. She didn't allow me to accompany her. She told me to stay and rest my heart. She had never before indicated that she knew about my heart trouble. I washed up and changed into some of Vincent's clothes. I sat at Vincent's desk and turned on his computer game. I don't know what I was looking for, maybe for some hidden message that would give me a clue to his whereabouts. It was Kara's belief that Frederick had kidnapped Vincent. But there was no clue on the computer, only the same old World War III. And the strange lights that came when the war was over. I played the game through to the end just to see the lights. I was trying to figure out how the game was supposed to continue with them in the picture, when Kara interrupted me.

"He's not in the cave," she said.

She staggered into the room and plopped down on the chair beside me. She was through crying for the time, but she was still terribly distraught. She had insisted we burn the heart in the fireplace, although I wanted to save it for the police. The red stain from it still colored her hands.

"Maybe it's not as bad as it looks," I said.

"You don't know Frederick," she said.

"Tell me about him."

"I can't."

"Then you'll be telling the police about him."

"Is that a threat?" she asked, too spent to be angry.

"It's a good idea. Whoever this guy is, he's got to be weird. I don't understand you, Kara. I'm worried."

"The police can't help us."

"You don't know that," I said. "Give them a chance."

"You don't understand."

"Christ!" I swore, slapping my leg. "I am sick and

tired of hearing remarks like that. You don't know. You don't understand. Only I know. *What* do you know? And what are you saving this knowledge up for? Vincent's welcome-home party? If this Frederick is as wicked as you and that mess on the counter indicate, then you won't be having that party soon, sister, unless you start talking to me or the police right now."

Kara looked at me with exhausted eyes. "You're right, Mark. It's time to tell all."

I sat back in my chair, surprised. "Who's Frederick?"

"It's a long story," she replied, not being evasive this time, her eyes straying to the game. Surprise crossed her face when she saw the lights gathered about the space station. "He put in the ships."

"Yes," I said. "Vincent said they were important."

"They are." Kara smiled faintly at the irony of something that I hoped she would soon reveal. "Everything is important. There is a reason for everything. Do you believe that, Mark?"

"On a good day."

She nodded. "You're like me in that way. You need proof, something you can see with your own eyes. Vincent's not like that. He trusts in the moment. He knows everything's going to be fine, and even if it isn't, he doesn't mind." She paused, a brief spasm of grief causing her right cheek to twitch. "But I shouldn't talk about the differences between you two. You both have incredible imaginations. You can imagine the strangest things and then bring them to life in your games, making them seem perfectly believable. I'm curious, Mark, were you ever able to win Vincent's game?"

"No. That's the problem with it. There is no way to win."

"Oh, but there is a way."

"What is it?" I asked.

She stared at the lights again. She appeared indecisive. "Never mind. I have to tell you about Frederick and Vincent and me."

"Please," I said, my impatience growing as rapidly as my concern. I didn't know why I hadn't called the police while she was hiking to the cave. In kidnappings I knew time was of the essence.

Kara nodded again at my prompting. She appeared to be on the verge of starting her tale when she suddenly reached out and touched my knee.

"How do you feel?" she asked.

"Horrible."

"What do you mean? Are you sick?"

"No. But with what's going on, how could I feel anything but horrible?"

"You don't feel dizzy or anything?" she asked. "Like you did when we were all together at the telescope?"

"No."

"You're sure?"

"Yes."

She relaxed slightly. "At least we have that going for us."

"I don't think I'm the one we should be worried about right now."

Kara gazed straight into my eyes. She had removed her contacts. I wondered if they had just been another prop, like her Scottish accent. Maybe now she no longer felt the need for them. Her eyes were no longer bright blue, but soft brown.

"That's not true," she said. "How you feel matters most of all."

"Who is Frederick?" I asked, tired of the riddles.

"My husband."

"What?"

"He's my husband, but Frederick's not his real name."

"Since when are you married?"

"I've been married a long time," she said.

I tried to digest the news. "This is some kind of joke, right?"

"No joke," she said.

"How old are you?"

"How old do I look?"

"My age," I said.

She considered a moment. "You could say that's a fair estimate." Then she changed the subject without expanding on the matter. "Mark, I have a story to tell you. Could you please just listen to it and not ask me what it has to do with our predicament until I finish?"

"What kind of story is it?"

"A science-fiction one."

"Don't tell me. You're from another planet. You're an alien whose flying saucer has run out of plutonium fuel. You need my help to break into a nuclear-power plant and steal uranium rods from the core so that you can get back home."

Kara was not amused. "What if that was my story? What would you do?"

"Nothing. I'd call the police and tell them that I

believe a friend of mine has been kidnapped. But I'd probably keep an eye on you from then on."

Kara sighed. "The story I have to tell you is far stranger than the one of your alien."

"Is it a true story?" I asked.

"It depends on your point of view."

"Don't play games with me, Kara."

"I don't mean to, but my story is much like Vincent's game. Only it starts before World War Three. It's about a woman and two men. I have to tell it mainly from the woman's point of view. Could you please just listen? Please, Mark?"

"I'm listening," I said.

Kara stared out over the city. Even with the normal layer of Los Angeles smog, it looked peaceful. Of course a thousand people were murdered in L.A. each year. One more death was not going to change the destiny of the world, I thought. It was a bitter thought, a result of the frustration I felt at just sitting and doing nothing while Vincent was in danger.

"There was this girl," Kara began. "She was intelligent, pretty—she had a lot going for her. She had big plans for her life. She was going to go to college, then medical school. She planned to be a famous doctor and help people the world over. And she did end up attending college, but she never became a doctor. She married too young, to a man who was also ambitious, too ambitious to have time for his wife's dreams. It's an old story, I know, but it's also new. It happens all the time.

"Anyway, she married this guy and played the role of the good wife while he joined the service. I realize that doesn't sound like the beginning of an exciting career—signing up for a stretch in the air force. But this woman's husband was smart. The air force recognized his abilities. They sent him to school, and he earned degrees in both nuclear engineering and aeronautics. He rose swiftly through the ranks: lieutenant, captain, colonel. He was hardly forty when they made him a general. It seemed that nothing could stop his rise to power.

"Except maybe his wife. His wife was not happy. It's hard to say why. Being the wife of a general carries many benefits with it. She had a nice house, plenty of money, and friends, but she didn't love her husband. I guess that's reason enough not to be happy. What's even sadder is that she probably never loved him, not even when she married him. But if anyone asked her why she didn't divorce him, she couldn't have answered. She had a feeling, though, even before her thirtieth birthday, that it was already too late for her. That she would never be happy, no matter what she did.

"The husband was not satisfied with the marriage either. He knew his wife didn't love him, and it drove him crazy. But he wasn't any better. He didn't love her either. He didn't love anybody. He was too busy to love anyone. He had to save the world from the enemy. He was a military man to the core. As far as he was concerned, there was always an enemy out there somewhere to be destroyed.

"Still, he was extremely attached to his wife. He couldn't make a decision without her. But he never listened to her. I know this sounds contradictory. He would get an opinion from her, then argue with her for several days about how foolish that opinion was, and then do exactly what he wanted, regardless of what his wife recommended. Then, if things didn't work out, he would blame her for confusing him with all her talk. He blamed her for everything all the time, for stalling his career at every juncture. Even though he was a general in his early forties, he was far from satisfied. He wanted to be the most powerful man on earth. He wanted to be president of the United States.

"He didn't make it to president. But when he was in his late fifties, he was put in command of America's third space station. There had been two prior to this one, but they didn't count for the general because they weren't armed. They had no missiles, no destructive lasers. But this new space station was loaded to the max. All by itself, it could have taken out the whole world.

"I have to pause here to say something about the political climate of the day. In a sense, it was better than what we have in our present society. Russia was an ally of the United States. China was the only major communist country left. There were far fewer missiles. Today the overkill on both sides is what? Tenfold? It's at least that. In this story the overkill was down to perhaps two times. Disarmament programs had succeeded in shrinking the stockpiles for thirty years. It gave the world a false sense of security. As a wise man once pointed out, you only need one bullet to blow someone's brains out. So we could only blow each other up once? We would still be dead.

"Anyway, this space station was supposed to be a secret, a kind of hidden life-insurance policy. God only knows who thought up the idea, but our general was its biggest supporter. The armaments aboard the station were deftly hidden. Officially, it was a scientific facility. What a joke. The missiles may have been hidden from the American people, but they were well known to the other side. And the space station made the other side very uneasy. For God's sake, it drifted right over China several times a day.

"Through quiet diplomatic channels, China tried to have it brought down. They were having enough troubles at home and didn't want a major confrontation. Our side said no, or rather, they denied there were arms on board. Of course, they wouldn't let the enemy board this innocent scientific facility to see how unarmed and safe it was.

"I say that sarcastically. In a way the space station was safer than any place on earth. Its lasers could destroy any incoming missiles, and it had a respectable force field that, once activated, made the station all but impervious to laser attack. Our general felt quite secure riding in it among the stars. He felt so secure he even brought his wife up to join him. Maybe he had begun to get a little worried about what he and his like-minded cohorts had started rolling down on good old planet earth. The other side refused to let the space station question rest. They issued an ultimatum: Take down that damn space station. You know how ultimatums are. They make everyone nervous. People do weird things when they're nervous. They don't think clearly. They begin to think things they've never thought before.''

"Someone pushed the button?" I interrupted.

Kara nodded with effort. "Yes."

"Who?"

"I don't know. Their side. Our side. Does it matter?"

"What happened?" I asked.

Kara shrugged. Her voice came out weak. "There was a war and everyone died."

"Like in Vincent's game?"

"Yes."

"Did the space station survive the war undamaged?"

"No," Kara said. "It was damaged, and several crew members died in the battle. The force field didn't work as well as it was supposed to. The hull was breached in two places. Some people were swept right out into space. A few others were burned to cinders in seconds. But the station survived. The other two stations—the actual scientific establishments—did not. They were blown out of the sky in the first five minutes of the war. They didn't stand a chance."

Kara paused again. Throughout her narration, she had kept her eyes fixed on the view out Vincent's bedroom window. She didn't look away now, but somehow, watching her as I was, I had the uncanny sensation that her view was no longer the same as mine. She was seeing the city through entirely different eyes. Nothing she had said had upset me. It was just a story, after all. But this look on her face disturbed me in ways the bloody heart in the kitchen had not. It was a look of total despair.

"The world was dead, Mark," she said finally. "Oh, there were some people alive, walking around down there, but they were goners. If the radiation didn't kill them, the coming ice age would. It would come fast. The bombs had thrown so much dust and smoke into the air that the people in the station couldn't even get a glimpse of the earth anymore. Yet there were these eerie orange glows in places. It was the fires burning beneath the smoke. There was no one to put them out. They just kept burning and burning, and you would stare at one of them and wonder if it was Paris or London or Los Angeles . . .''

Kara began to cry softly. I left her in peace. I couldn't very well console her by telling her that none of it had happened. She knew that. She wasn't crazy. But I did begin to wonder if the shock of Vincent's kidnapping had momentarily thrown her. I believed in the kidnapping. I had a burned heart lying in the fireplace for evidence.

But that look on Kara's face wouldn't go away. Nor would the disquiet it brought to my own heart. It was amazing, I thought, what she had said about the radiation and the ice age. Vincent had said the same things when he had first shown me his game—almost word for word. Another coincidence. They kept piling up like a growing snowball rushing out of control toward a blazing fire. Something had to break. I could feel it. Either the fires Kara was weeping over had to be put out or the snow would come, and never mind that in her story one brought the other.

"Kara," I said finally, gently, after a couple of minutes had gone by. "We've got to find Vincent."

She nodded and sniffed once. "We can find him."

"Do you know where he is?"

"No. You do."

"Huh?" I said.

"You can locate him."

"How?"

"I have to finish my story. Then you'll understand."

"But we don't have time for it right now."

"Please, Mark, you promised me you'd listen."

I took a deep breath and counted to ten as the psychologists recommend. I could have counted to a hundred and turned blue and my anxiety still wouldn't have gone away. "Go on," I told her.

Kara sat up straight in her chair and gave me her full attention. Apparently the city no longer interested her, and I think it was because in her story it was no longer there. As she wiped away her tears, I thought how weird it was that I had taken only a moment to get used to her eyes being brown instead of blue. It was as if they had always been brown and I just hadn't noticed.

"The space station remained largely intact," she said. "About one hundred people survived. A shuttle had been docked to the station at the outbreak of the war, but the battle had damaged it beyond repair. It didn't matter. There was nowhere left to land it, and even if there had been, there was no point. The people on the station were alone. They knew they were doomed. The station was large. It was powered by nuclear fusion. It had gardens aboard for growing food and replenishing the air supply, but the station was not self-sufficient. It needed regular supplies from below under the best of conditions, and with the vast loss of oxygen that occurred when the hull was breached, the people aboard could count the days till they smothered. They began to count. One day. Two days. One week. The time passed slowly. That's how it is when you're waiting to die."

"Did some commit suicide?" I asked, trying to show I was listening. Kara nodded.

"Some," she said. "But not many. Bad as things got, most of the people never gave up. They kept waiting—I can't say what for. There was this feeling that pervaded the space station that it simply couldn't end this way. It wasn't right that humanity should just disappear. It was hopeless—yes, we all knew that. Yet we had hope."

"We?"

She nodded again. "We."

"Who is we?" I asked as carefully as I could.

"Me and the others."

"You were aboard this space station?"

"Yes," she said, not blinking.

"What were you doing there?"

"I was married to the commander of the station."

"I see," I said.

"You don't have to believe me now, Mark. I don't mind."

"Thank you."

"Should I continue?"

I shifted uneasily. "If you want."

"Do you ever pray?" she asked.

"Very seldom."

"Who do you pray to when you do pray?"

"God," I said.

"But usually only when you have a problem, right?"

"Yeah, I suppose. I don't think about it a lot."

"Well, we had a problem. By the second week our air had gone bad. It stunk. You'd take a deep breath and feel like you got nothing out of it. You'd want to take another one right away, but you knew the effort was using up more oxygen than the deep breath was giving you in return. It was hard to be alive.

"What happened, finally, was that everyone gathered in the hub of the station. The space was cramped, but at least at the hub there was no gravity. You can squeeze a lot of people in a small room when they can float on top of one another. It was getting near the end. Some people were already beginning to lose consciousness. We figured we had maybe another six hours before we passed out. We had a discussion—it was really quite beautiful. We decided that we would pray until we died. Not to be saved, but to say we were sorry for having destroyed our world. Now, someone might view that cynically. Naturally we would not pray to be saved. There was no chance. Still, you had to have been there. We were all scared. None of us wanted to die. We could say what we wanted, but none of us knew what to expect on the other side, or if there even was another side. Nevertheless, we chose what I thought a dignified way to go out. We accepted our portion of the blame for what had happened. We accepted our punishment."

"Did your husband take part in this prayer?" I asked.

"No. He was too busy."

"Go on."

Kara closed her eyes. "I remember that time as if it were happening to me right now. Our prayer was mainly within—we didn't have much breath left to speak it out loud. We were all Americans, of course, but there were a variety of races aboard the station, a variety of beliefs. When we first began, some prayed aloud, in different tongues. I remember how the sound blended together and became one sound, one voice talking to God. It was very special, but sad, very sad, too.

"Then everything began to settle down. The six hours began to pass. Except for the wheeze of labored breathing, there was silence. I think I dozed for a while. I drifted from my spot to the end of the hub. There the station was equipped with wide circular windows. When I opened my eyes I could see the moon. It was full, and as the station rotated on its axis, the moon appeared to go up and down, up and down. It was hypnotic. It was like staring up at the moon in the nighttime sky while riding on the arm of an oil well."

"What did you say?" I asked, startled.

Kara opened her eyes. "An oil well. The kind that goes up and down. You know?"

"That's what Becky did when we were out on our date. She jumped on an oil well and almost got herself killed."

Kara was not surprised. She closed her eyes again. "I can still see that," she said. "It was a last impression. It went deep. It was near the end. The air was almost gone. I could hear each breath drag through my chest as if I were old and ill. I was old then. I could hear my heart. The beats were slowing down. The time between each one seemed to take as long as it took for the moon to come up again. But I had my eyes open. I was conscious. I had stopped praying. I was thinking about my life. I was thinking about you.''

"Me?"

"Yes."

"Why would you think about me?" I asked.

"I remembered you."

"From when?"

"From long ago." Kara opened her eyes. "Look at me, Mark. Who do you see?"

"Kara."

"And who is Kara?"

"I don't know." A cold sweat had sprung out on my forehead. Suddenly I had the inexplicable sensation of being cornered and lost at the same time. "You're my friend."

"How did you feel when you met me?"

"Why are you asking me this?"

"How did you feel, Mark?"

I paused. "As if I knew you."

"You did know me, even though you didn't recognize me. I knew you wouldn't. I took precautions. I dyed my hair. I bought contacts. I changed my voice. I wore makeup that changed the contours of my face ever so slightly. But I think if I had done none of those things, you still wouldn't have recognized me. I don't think any of us can see something we don't believe is possible. Do you understand?"

"No."

"Did Becky ever tell you her first name?"

"No," I said.

"She would never tell anybody."

"That's right," I mumbled. I was having trouble breathing. The dimensions of the room seemed to have altered. The walls were closing in on me, while at the same time they were dissolving into a nothingness that stretched forever. I glanced anxiously to the right and the left to reassure myself I was where I was supposed to be. Suddenly I was afraid to look at Kara. Just the sight of her filled me with terror.

"Look at me, Mark. Who do you see?"

It was like a mystical command. I didn't want to obey, but I had to obey. My head turned in her direction. She leaned forward so her face was only inches from mine, and her eyes were all I could see. Those sweet brown eyes that had caught my attention the moment I walked into the record store.

"Oh, God," I whispered.

"Do you know what Becky's first name is?"

"Kara."

"That's right." Kara nodded and sat back in her chair. "I'm Becky. I'm from the future, Mark. I've come back for you."

CHAPTER ELEVEN

It would be shameful for me to say I knew all along. It would, in another sense, also be correct. I was completely infatuated with Becky when I met Kara. But even when I became infatuated with Kara, I *consciously* understood that there was no conflict. I just didn't stop to think about why I felt no conflict. That's all. I never stopped to look at Kara. I never stopped to look at Becky, for that matter. I was too busy daydreaming about them. That's how it is for me with the people I love. They become unreal to me. I guess I like them better that way.

Still, now I had a *real* problem. I believed Kara all right, without a shadow of a doubt. The eyes, the voice, the face, the body—everything was the same. But she was talking about time travel and I hadn't even bothered to write a time travel computer game because the topic was simply too far out. My mind quickly jumped to the possibility of Becky's having an identical twin. Just as quickly I discarded it. Kara knew Becky as no twin could know a sister. They were the same person, I knew, and the laws of physics were simply going to have to understand.

What did I do when she made her incredible revelation? I just stared at the floor and went straight to the heart of the matter.

"Who's going to win the World Series in the year two thousand and ten?" I asked.

Kara nodded. "You believe me."

"I don't know."

"It's me, Mark. It's Becky."

"What are you doing this Saturday night?"

She didn't smile. "I won't be here."

"Are you going back to the future?"

"Not exactly." She glanced at her watch. "I have to finish my story."

"All right."

She was concerned. "Are you all right?"

"No. But you were about to die. Tell me what happened."

She closed her eyes again, and as she did so, she looked older. Not physically, of course, but the experiences she had gone through were there in her face, her voice. I tried not to think about what that meant. I hadn't always been happy during my short stay on earth, but I'd never blamed the planet. I didn't want it to die any more than I wanted Vincent to die.

I didn't stop to ask myself who Vincent was.

"I was staring at the moon and thinking of you,"

Kara began. "I was thinking about how you used to come into the record store and make me laugh. This wasn't the first time I had thought of you in all those years. During the first few years of my marriage, I'd sometimes sit and daydream about you for hours. I used to wonder where you were, what you were doing. I did that until I was about thirty."

"Why did you stop?"

Kara looked uncomfortable. She kept her eyes closed. "That'll become clear as I go along," she said.

"OK," I said, not reassured by her response.

"The moon appears brighter seen from space. You would know this. The light doesn't have to go all the way through the earth's atmosphere. Staring at it as I was, however, it suddenly appeared as bright as the sun, which it never does, even in deep space. Yet the light did not hurt my eyes. I can't explain why. It was a cool white light. It blotted out everything else, even my fear of death. It seemed to surround the entire space station, to fill my head. All I could see, all I knew, was this great white light. And I felt such joy then. I can't tell you how it was. Everything was fine. Everything was perfect. It was the Illumni."

"The what?" I asked.

Kara opened her eyes. "You mean, the who. The Illumni are a superior race from another star system."

I sighed. "I knew aliens were going to come into this somehow."

Kara laughed softly. "The Illumni are not like the aliens you see in science-fiction movies. They don't even have bodies. They have evolved beyond a need for physical form.''

"But what was this light you saw? Their bodies?"

"Their ships."

"Why do they need ships if they don't have bodies?"

Kara paused. "I never thought of that. It doesn't matter. They were there to help us."

"They should have come a few weeks earlier."

"They said they couldn't. They didn't say why. Anyway, I take that back. They weren't there to help us, but to give us the chance to help ourselves. This is important to understand. The Illumni do not think the same as we do. I don't know if they even have thoughts as we do. I'm not even sure they have individuality as we understand individuality. It didn't matter which one I communicated with—it was as if I was talking with all of them at the same time."

"They spoke English?" I asked.

"I use the word *talking* loosely. The Illumni communicate telepathically." Kara smiled. "It's difficult to describe what it's like to make mental contact with them. It's so incredibly delightful. You feel like you're with your best friend. You can say—I mean, you can think—anything, and they'll understand."

"How many did you personally communicate with?"

Kara paused again. "Only one, I believe."

"Then how can you say that communicating with one was like communicating with them all?" I asked.

"That was the impression I received when I talked with the other humans about the experience afterward. Is something wrong?"

"I was simply entertaining the idea that there may have been only one of them," I said.

"No, there were definitely many. Close to a hundred I'd say. But you've raised an interesting issue. I can't overemphasize this. From their point of view, everything is the same, everything is one. I know that sounds like a trite philosophical concept, but when you're with them, in contact with them, it seems the highest of truths, the answer to all questions. But they told us that this state of unity is not something that can be imagined. What I mean is, without the Illumni present, it's a meaningless idea."

"Do they have a God?"

"I never asked them."

"Why not?" I asked.

"It never occurred to me. What do you think so far?"

"I'm intrigued, Becky."

She made a face. "Don't call me that. I hate that name."

"Why did you hate the name Kara when you were younger?"

"I didn't. I loved it. I loved it so much that I only wanted those who truly loved me to know it."

"That's bizarre. Please go on with your story."

"The Illumni saved us for the time being," Kara said. "They restored our oxygen supply. They went a big step further than that. They took a small part of the earth that had been totally devastated in the war and made it whole again, with trees and rivers and hills to walk in. They transported us there. They gave us a tiny paradise where we could rest for a while and heal ourselves from the trauma of the war."

"Where on earth was this place?"

"Right here."

"Los Angeles?" I asked.

"Yes. Why? Does that surprise you?"

"Because you grew up in L.A. Were you the one who chose the spot?"

"No. But why shouldn't it have been here? Here is as good a place as any."

"I suppose. It just strikes me as an amazing coincidence."

"Other people aboard the station also grew up in Los Angeles."

"Fine," I said. "I shouldn't keep interrupting."

"I don't mind. You have such a sharp intellect. Your questions help me understand the whole thing better." Kara glanced out the window in the direction of our path into the hills and the secret cave. She smiled again and now it seemed the memory of better days was at hand.

"The Illumni are miracle workers," she continued. "You probably know this, but the Los Angeles basin, with all its aerospace industries, is a prime target in a war. This place was hit with God knows how many warheads. No one survived, and the hills you see here were burned to ash. But in a matter of days the Illumni caused them to bloom with grass and flowers. You should have seen the trees. They grew with each passing hour, with long slender blue and green and red branches. The leaves were like individual watercolor paintings. I used to pluck them and carry a handful as I went for my walks—they smelled like flowers. Even when they dropped to the ground, they never shriveled and died. It was like being in heaven."

"What did your general husband think of all this?" I asked.

"I didn't spend much time with him after the Illumni arrived."

"You went to court and got a divorce?"

"Had there been a court left standing I would have. But, no, I was busy with someone else. Do you know who that was?"

"Vincent," I said.

"In a manner of speaking. Mark, now we come to a very delicate subject. It's important that what I tell you next doesn't upset you. This is what happened but it's not what has to happen."

"I doubt anything could upset me after World War Three."

"How about your future?"

I shrugged. "I assume I went up in flames with everyone else."

Kara's expression was grave. "You weren't alive for World War Three."

I swallowed. I felt kind of sick. "That's OK. I never liked fighting anyway." Then I considered a moment. "Wait a second. How do you know what happened to me? You never had contact with me."

"The Illumni told me."

"How did they know?" I asked.

"They know everything."

129

"Are you serious? Everything?"

"I shouldn't say that," Kara replied. "I can't speak for them. But their knowledge seemed to me to have no limits. However, it was not as if they answered every question put to them. Half the time they didn't respond one way or the other."

"But they told you about me?"

"Yes."

"How old was I when I died?" I asked.

"It doesn't have to be this way, Mark. It shouldn't be this way."

"How old?"

"Twenty-nine."

I coughed. "The good always die young."

"Mark."

"Was it my heart?"

"Yes," Kara said.

"You've known about my heart?"

"Yes."

I nodded. I believed her. Actually, when I thought about it, I was surprised I'd made it that long. Twenty-nine. Christ, I had only about ten years left.

Then it really hit me, and it was not something I could laugh off. My eyes started to get all teary. It was totally humiliating. I didn't want to cry in front of Kara. But this horribly sad feeling swept over me right then, as cold as a gust of wind blowing off a glacier. I'd had it before, but not this bad. I wanted my mother. She had given me life, and now I wanted her to stop the future from taking my life away. But my mother was not there. She had never been there for me. Neither had my father. All I had was Kara. She reached for my hand and I let her take it and stroke it. I wanted to stop trembling. Only I couldn't stop trembling any more than I could have willed my heart to beat when it wanted to stop. My chest suddenly felt constricted, and I was afraid my heart was going to stop right then, that I was going to die in my girlfriend's arms before I had a chance to be her boyfriend.

But I didn't die. Kara held on to me, and slowly my premature grave was covered over in my mind and I was able to sit straight and not shake. I wiped at my face. I was embarrassed.

"I'm sorry," I said.

"It's OK," she said, her face pressed close to mine.

"It just hit me all of a sudden."

"I understand."

I forced a chuckle. "You know what they say about someone walking over your grave."

"No one's going to walk over yours," Kara promised, sitting back in her chair. "You're not going to die at twenty-nine. Let me continue with my story. While we walked in our tiny corner of paradise, the Illumni came to us with an offer, a chance to save our world."

"By going back in time?" I asked, my breathing still not steady. I couldn't get rid of the feeling that I had just seen my tombstone, complete with inscribed dates.

"Yes. They made us a fascinating offer. They said

we could go back to any point in our lives for exactly one lunar cycle—approximately one month—and try to change the course of our lives in such a way that the history of the world would also be changed. Remember, we're talking about fewer than a hundred people. It was—is—a tall order. Particularly since we were forbidden to try to convince the populace as a whole that we were from the future. For example, we can't bring out technology from the future or take advantage of the stock market or such things. We were told we had to work in secret.''

"Did they tell you what would happen if you didn't?"

"No. But I received the impression it would be a serious mistake."

"But your telling me this story is a violation of that order."

"It wasn't an order," Kara said. "The Illumni never order anything. They cherish free will above all else. It was simply strong advice." Kara paused, worried. "Do you think I've gone against their advice? You're not the population."

"If they're as highly evolved as you say, I'm sure they'll forgive you."

Kara thought for a moment before continuing, tugging on her beautiful blond hair, which I now knew was really brown.

"Yeah," she said. "Anyway, I was alone on a hill when my Illumni made this offer. It both excited and depressed me. I didn't know what to do, which Becky to go back to. The Illumni really wanted us to influence, not the world, but the world through an earlier version of ourselves. Do you understand?"

"Yes. They wanted you to take care of yourself first."

"Exactly. I expressed my confusion to the Illumni. I can't say she told me what to do, but I do believe she guided me."

"She?" I asked.

"Yes. I think it was a she."

"The Illumni don't have bodies but they have gender?"

"Yes," Kara said. "What's wrong with that?"

"I don't know. I've never met an alien."

"Someday you will. As I was saying, the Illumni guided me in the direction of love. What could I do that would bring greater love to the world? This question seemed the only one worth asking. You see what I'm getting at? Before I opened myself up to this guidance, when I thought about how to save the world, my mind naturally went to the different ways to bring about greater peace between the superpowers. But in the Illumni's presence, such ideas appeared childish. I knew I couldn't go back in time and get Becky to quit her job at the record store and join a protest group." Kara paused. "Then you came to mind. I thought, what if I had married you instead of Ray?"

"You married Ray?" I asked, startled.

"Yes. He was the general. I thought you knew that by now."

"I didn't."

"You look shocked," Kara said.

"He's a jerk."

"I know," she said.

"Why did you marry him?"

"I made a mistake."

I shook my head. "This alien and time travel stuff—maybe I believe you. But Becky getting married to Ray—that's horrible."

"Are you disappointed in me?"

"Yes."

Kara looked hurt. "Well, you didn't offer to marry me."

"What are you talking about? You wouldn't even go out with me."

"You asked me at a bad time."

"I asked you a dozen times," I said.

"If you had dressed a little better when you came into the store, maybe I would have said yes."

"Becky doesn't care how I dress."

"*I'm* Becky, Mark. *I* care."

I stopped. "You have a point there. You really didn't like the way I dressed?"

"I told you. You looked as if your mother had bought your clothes."

"OK. Enough," I said. "I need a black leather jacket and a black Ferrari. What were we talking about?"

"Who I should have married. When I was with the Illumni, I thought that if I could go back in time and somehow get Becky together with you, I could change my life for the better and thereby make the world a better place."

"And then there wouldn't be a war?" I asked.

"Yes."

"That sounds a little farfetched to me."

"The Illumni didn't seem to think so," Kara said.

"Why did you think I would make such a difference in your life? Was it just a feeling?"

"It was a feeling and something more," Kara said. "Before coming back to this time, I had a chance to spend time with you."

"What? When? I thought the deal was that you could only go back in time once?"

"I got to spend time with you after the war."

"But I was dead," I protested.

"You were dead. You were dead and buried. But you were buried in a special manner. Mark, do you know how people sometimes have themselves frozen after they're dead in the hope that in the future a way will be found to revive them?"

"Yes. It's a ridiculous idea."

Kara hesitated. "Why?"

"Because of what is known as the 'ice barrier.' Practically every liquid in the universe shrinks when it is frozen. Water's unique. It expands. The human body is largely composed of water. When people have themselves frozen, the water in every cell in their bodies expands and ruptures every cell wall. These people don't simply need to be thawed out and revived, they need to be regrown."

"What if I were to tell you that ten years from now this ice barrier will be overcome?" Kara asked.

"Is that true? Was this discovery made before the war?"

"It must have been."

"Was it or wasn't it?" I asked. "If the discovery was made, you would have read about it."

Kara looked doubtful. "I didn't read about it, but then, I didn't keep up with science, except as far as it influenced Ray's career. But if there is an ice barrier, as you say, then it must have been overcome."

"How can you be sure?" I asked.

"When you died, you had yourself frozen," Kara said.

"I did? I did not. I would never do that. The idea disgusts me."

"Would it disgust you if you knew there was a chance you could be successfully revived in a future time when your heart defect could be fixed?"

"Yes," I said.

"Don't give me a hard time."

"A hard time? I'm the one you're turning into a Popsicle here."

"It happened, Mark."

It wasn't fair, I thought, having to argue with someone from the future. "All right," I said. "I had myself frozen. Obviously I defrosted when the bombs went off."

"Not at all. All frozen bodies were kept above the Arctic Circle. You were unaffected."

"Why?"

"It's cold up there," Kara said simply.

"Wait a second. What are you getting at here? Did your Illumni thaw me out so you could have another look at me and decide whether you wanted to go to the movies with me after all?"

"More or less. But it wasn't my Illumni who did the actual revival. It was another."

"Why?"

"I don't know."

"How old were you when I was defrosted?" I asked.

Kara hit me. "You have a nerve. You were a corpse! I looked great well into my fifties."

"I've always liked older women. How did I look?"

"Like Vincent."

"I don't understand."

"Yes, you do," Kara said.

Another time to stop and reflect. Another time to feel the pain in my chest, to cry at what might have been and what would be. But I did none of these things. Instead, I smiled, all the way down into my heart. I smiled because I had adored Vincent the moment I met him. Because he was so neat. I didn't mind that I'd become like him. There was no one else I could think of that I would want to be.

Kara nodded in understanding. She was reading my mind again. The Illumni had obviously taught her a trick or two.

"I understand," I said.

"It was fun walking in these hills with you."

I was embarrassed. "I bet Ray loved it."

A shadow fell across Kara's face. "He didn't. But not until I saw that bloody heart in the kitchen did I understand how much it must have bothered him."

"Was there no one he wanted the Illumni to thaw out?"

137

"Please don't joke about this, Mark."

"I'm sorry."

"I have very little left to say, but what I have left is crucial," Kara went on. "With you by my side, my decision to return to the time that you first entered my life became even more apparent. Vincent agreed to go with me. Together we made plans to get you and Becky together."

Something about that didn't ring true. "But Vincent didn't approve of your plan to sabotage Becky's relationship with Ray."

"Why do you say that?" Kara asked.

"I thought it was obvious. He never really supported it."

Kara frowned. "He supported it."

I shrugged. "You'd know better than I."

"Maybe not. You're Vincent." Kara shook her head. "We talked about it and he said he wanted us to be together for our whole lives."

"Maybe it was just the way you went about it that he didn't like. You know, trying to make the end justify the means and all that stuff."

"I don't know what you mean," Kara said, and I believed I might have insulted her.

"You sort of pressed the issue," I said as delicately as I could.

"What would you have done? I had only a month."

"I don't know," I said.

"No. Tell me. I want to know."

"Did you ask Vincent what he would have done?"

"I told you, we discussed it," Kara said.

"Yes. But did you ask his opinion?"

"Of course." Kara hesitated. "Well, he knew what I was going to do. He didn't try to stop me."

"Maybe he didn't want to interfere with your free will," I said, the strangest feeling coming over me at the comment, as if I had just solved the riddle once and for all. A pity I didn't know what the riddle was. "Please finish your story."

"Very well," Kara said, apparently content to let the matter rest. "We decided to go back to a month ago from today. I felt that Becky would have known you long enough by then. And if a bad situation were to arise between her and Ray, she'd go out with you. The Illumni told us that when we came back we'd be the same age as you two. It makes sense, I suppose. The Illumni had no inhibitions about giving us spending money for our trip. We brought back a sack of precious gems. Vincent and I sold them right away and bought this house and the cars."

"Do you know the principle upon which their time machine works?"

"No."

"Damn." I was disappointed. "Not even a clue?"

Kara smiled. "Have you seen *The Wizard of Oz?*"

"Who hasn't?"

"Remember the part at the end when the good witch helps Dorothy to return home? Dorothy closes her eyes and repeats, 'There's no place like home. There's no place like home.' Basically that's what we did. We focused our minds on this time. We had to do it in that cave on the hill. Maybe that's where the

Illumni keep their time machine. Vincent and I came into this time from out of that cave. I remember it was a sunny day. The city was alive with millions of people. It was great to be back."

"Is the Illumni time machine present in the cave now?" I asked.

Kara raised an eyebrow. "An interesting question. I never thought about it. We never actually saw it before we left, although we felt it at work. I suppose it could be there even now. The inside of the cave does have a timeless quality about it."

"Wait a second, I'm confused. If the time machine is not there, how are you going to get back to the future?"

"I'm not going back," Kara said.

"But you spoke of going away on a long trip. Weren't you talking about returning to the future?"

"No. Do you know what it means to violate causality?"

I was familiar with the topic from all the science fiction I had read. It was the main problem scientists had with the concept of time travel. It was why they thought it was impossible. Simply put, the problem read: How can something go back to the past and affect its future in such a way as to prevent its backward journey through time? Science-fiction writers tended to phrase the dilemma by asking how someone could go back in time and kill his own grandmother. If the man in question kills his grandmother at a young enough age, then his own mother will never be born, and then he'll never be born. The end result being, of course, that it would then be impossible for him to kill his grandmother in the first place. It all got very confusing.

"Yes," I told Kara. "I'm familiar with the paradoxes. But from what you've said, the Illumni are giving you a chance to change what's to be, and never mind how the future is affected."

"That's right," she said. "But think what that means. There can be only one Kara in the future. She'll be someone else. I hope she'll be a happier Kara in a happier world. But there'll be nowhere for me to go *back* to."

"But what will happen to you?" I asked.

"I will cease to exist."

"When?"

"When the moon is full."

"The moon is full tonight!"

"I know."

I was upset. "You're going to die?"

Kara smiled sadly. "I don't think there's any death, not anymore. In some time, someplace, I'll always be alive. Don't grieve for me, Mark. We're going to be spending the rest of our lives together."

"But it won't be with the you who's you," I protested.

"What would you prefer? The future I lived? The one you didn't get a chance to live?"

"I'll still die when I'm twenty-nine," I said. "Becky's not a heart surgeon. She can't save me."

"The Illumni don't agree. They say the ultimate cause of physical weakness is unhappiness. You'll be happy with Becky."

"But the defect in my heart is congenital," I said. "It's not simply going to go away."

"I didn't say it would. But you have the defect now and you're alive. The reason you died at the age of twenty-nine was that the loneliness of your life finally wore you down. Trust me on this. Trust the Illumni. With me in your life, your heart will go on beating for many years to come."

I shook my head. "I can't believe you're just going to be gone."

Kara was reflective. "Neither can I."

"When exactly will it happen?"

"I'm not sure."

"Will you just dissolve?" I asked.

"I honestly don't know."

"Are you scared?"

"I'm scared of Frederick and what he's done," Kara said. "Fred is Ray's middle name. They're the same person. He's obviously come back to wreck my plans."

"Why?" I asked.

"The Illumni must have given him an opportunity to try to save the world also. I'm sure he would have jumped at it. But you've got to understand the Ray I know. He's ruthlessly ambitious. Do you know what he said to me after the war, when the entire world lay in ruins? He said we should have hit China with everything we had as soon as our space station was assembled. Then we would have won decisively. That's the kind of mentality we're dealing with. He only understands force. He sees an enemy everywhere, including in his own home. Throughout his career, he blamed me for his failure to become president. For God's sake, he wouldn't have made it to general without me! I think I see what he's come back for. He's determined to set Ray on what he believes is a straight road to the top. He wants to be president. He wants to be in a position to order a first strike. To do all this, he thinks he must keep Becky away from Ray."

"Don't you have that backward?" I asked. "He deliberately went to Ray and told him what we were up to."

Kara dismissed the objection with a wave of her hand. "He did that out of jealousy. He hates me now. He saw how I went off with Vincent. Don't think for a second that he's fighting to save me for himself. He hates you even more. That's why he came after Vincent."

"Why didn't he come after me directly?"

"He probably doesn't know where you live."

"How did Ray find Vincent so easily?" I asked.

"He may have come out of the cave and bumped right into him."

"Will he hurt Vincent?"

"I'm not sure," Kara said. "Ray was willing to destroy the lives of millions of people. The bloody heart he left in the kitchen doesn't exactly encourage me."

"Why did he do that?" I asked.

"To let me know he was on to me. To scare me."

"Why are we sitting here talking? We're wasting time. You said you knew where Ray took him. Let's go after him."

"I didn't say that. I said *you* knew where Vincent was."

"But I don't know."

"Of course you do. You're Vincent. That's how I know Frederick hasn't killed him yet. You would have felt it. But there's something more. Remember when you were looking through the telescope and your head brushed close to Vincent's? Remember your dizziness? That was the result of a momentary blending of your minds. The Illumni warned us about that. You notice I've had almost no contact with Becky. When two of the same person are together, all kinds of strange things can happen."

"But Vincent and I sat together for hours," I said.

"Vincent's mind is far more developed than mine. He's able to put up a wall against the blending. Even so, strange things happened to you guys on at least two occasions that I saw."

"What does this have to do with our predicament?"

Kara stood. "We're hiking up to the cave. Once we get there you're going to sit and close your eyes and get into Vincent's mind. It will be easy. He'll let you in. I'm sure he knows where Frederick has taken him. What he knows, you'll also know."

I climbed to my feet. I looked out the window. The day was moving on. Night would be coming soon, and with it the moon. There was a painful question that needed to be asked.

"Kara," I said. "If all you say is true, is it necessary to save Vincent? I don't mean to sound cruel, but he's going to be gone soon anyway."

Kara shook slightly at the question, but her eyes remained fixed on mine. "I can't leave without Vincent by my side. You asked earlier if I was scared. I didn't really answer your question. But I think you know the answer. You have to help me find him, Mark."

CHAPTER TWELVE

Inside the cave, in the inner chamber I had visited before, Kara lit her gas lantern against the oppressive dark. But no light penetrated the black hole at the rear of the chamber. No light penetrated my heart. I had to face my fears. I knew who I was. I was Mark Forum. Kara was asking me to be someone else. It did not matter that it was someone I loved. Kara understood. When we were comfortably seated, she tried to reassure me.

"The Illumni taught us that the cause of all fear is the presence of a second," she said. "What they mean is that if one sees any difference anywhere, there is always the possibility of danger. The Illumni don't fear anything because they are one with everything. I realize, of course, we can't pretend to be in that state of unity. But the fact that it exists gives me comfort. I hope it does the same for you. You are not going to experience anything foreign when you go into Vincent's mind.''

"Are you sure he'll let me in?" I asked.

"You're already in. It's merely a question of remembering what has yet to happen. What's the difference between you two? He's only had more experience than you, nothing more. Close your eyes, Mark; it will be easier that way.''

I did as she suggested. "What do I do?" I asked.

"Be still.''

"Do you want me to blank out my thoughts?"

"No. The Illumni say that's impossible. We can never force our minds to do anything. They'll do just the opposite. Try not to think and you'll have more thoughts. What you should do instead is give your mind something more pleasant to dwell on than what it is already caught up with. Then there will be no force involved. Be with the thought of Vincent, that's all. It's a pleasant thought. He's a great person. He's a more evolved form of your present self. Be easy, Mark, and imagine Vincent as you remember him. His smile, his carefree manner. Be with him. Be him.''

I began to protest. I was too wound up with all that was going on to relax. I wanted to jump up and run out of the cave and find a gun and hunt Frederick down. But just as the idea of arming myself passed through my mind, I couldn't help wondering what Vincent would have said. And no sooner did I wonder than I thought I heard him laugh. Or saw him smile at least. Then I suddenly did see him smile. It was so vivid he could have been standing in front of me. Or standing with his back to me, with me peering over his shoulder into a mirror.

Two mirrors, I corrected myself. Each placed in front of the other, with us between, reflecting back and forth down a tunnel of endlessly rebounding images. I saw them clearly. They took shape in my mind like pictures projected on the back of my eyelids. I felt myself step into one of the tunnels, a long dark passageway with a faint white light at the far end. I felt myself begin to fall, slowly at first, as if I had grown wings to help ease my descent. I was vaguely conscious of my body remaining in the cave beside Kara, but it seemed I had become so still I was no longer breathing. I had turned to stone.

I was aware of speed without the jarring effects of motion. I fell and fell down the long corridor, and with each passing second the light at the end grew brighter. But it was not a white light as I had thought at first. Nor was it exceedingly bright. At present the tunnel was not leading out of my body and into the presence of a glorious being. It was just leading me into another body.

Suddenly my descent stopped. I jumped without moving. My place with Kara was lost. The tunnel disappeared. I opened my eyes.

I was in a motel room. My hands and feet were bound. I was lying on the floor with my head pressed at an uncomfortable angle against a wall that needed paint. A dusty mirror on a chipped and splintered chest of drawers hung above me. I twisted my head to the right, feeling pain in my neck. There was someone on the bed.

It was Ray.

He was the same age as he was in the bookstore. His body language, however, was not that of a twenty-year-old kid. He had a cigar in his right hand, and the way he gestured with it as he talked was an exercise in arrogance. I'd disliked Ray when I watched him pick up Kara in his store, but this guy was worse. And to think he'd had five hundred warheads waiting at his fingertips.

He had, however, made a few changes in his appearance. His hair was lighter. He also appeared to be wearing contacts. I could not remember Ray's eyes being green. I tried to think of him as Frederick. It made it easier for me to keep everybody straight in my head.

The smoke from his cigar filled the room with a foul smell. I coughed weakly. My mouth was gagged with an old rag. It was difficult to breathe. I was in Vincent's body. But where was Vincent? Where were his fearless thoughts? I was alone.

"You know what's wrong with people like you?" Frederick was saying. "You only have guts when you don't need them. I've seen it a thousand times. You go to rallies and burn the American flag. But if a thief breaks into your home, suddenly you want a little frontier justice—someone with a gun. You call the cops. You should be able to take care of your own problems. That's what I do. You should have learned to take care of yourself. You see, Vincent, you're my problem now. That's the cold reality of the situation. What do you think I should do with you?"

I told him, through my gag, to go to hell. It came out like a pathetic mumble. Frederick took pity on me. Wearing a jovial sneer, he climbed from the bed and knelt by my head. He had on a black sport coat. I couldn't help but notice the slim switchblade tucked in his coat pocket.

"You speak?" he mocked me. "I thought you were beyond all insults."

I told him to go do something to himself that the Bible wouldn't have approved of. He got the gist of it. His face broke into a grin.

"Vincent, there's hope for you after all. If I remove your gag, do you promise not to scream? Neither of us would want that, would we? I would have to shut you up quick, and that could get kind of messy."

I nodded. He undid the rag at the back of my head. At last I could breathe freely.

"Hi," I said, cautioning myself to move carefully.

"What did you just say?"

"Nothing."

"Come on," he insisted. "What was it? You've bored me the whole day. Now you're going to talk."

"What would you like to talk about?"

"Where's your double?" he asked.

"Beats me."

He belted me in the face. He was every bit as strong as Ray, which made sense. Ten times as fierce. Twice in one day, I couldn't believe it. I tasted blood.

A numbing pain swelled in my head. I couldn't be sure, but it felt as if he'd broken my nose.

"Where is he?" he demanded.

"How should I know?" I gasped.

"You know I'm going to find him."

"What do you want him for?"

"I want to pull his arms out of their sockets. What do you think I want him for? You guys are trying to steal my wife."

"Your wife is trying to get away from you. Why don't you just let her go and we'll all be a lot happier."

Frederick grinned again. "I'm afraid I can't do that. There's this thing called pride. It's the difference between a guy like me and a guy like you. I have a lot of it. I couldn't live knowing she was with somebody else."

Kara *had* underestimated him. I realized then that he intended to kill Becky as well. It should have been obvious. What better way to keep Ray away from her while Ray moved toward the presidency?

"You won't find either of them," I swore at him, my own pride overcoming my earlier caution. "They've been warned. They'll hide until your month is up and you turn to dust."

Anger and doubt wiped away his grin. "You lie! Kara would never have gone against the Illumni. Even if she had, Becky would never have listened to her."

"Kara only told Mark the truth. He told Becky. She listened to him. She knows about you. You'll never find her."

Frederick was livid. He leapt to his feet and began to pace the floor. "I'll get Kara. She'll know where they are. I'll beat the information out of her if I have to.''

"You'll get nothing from her," I said. "She's too smart for you. She always has been. Without Kara, Ray will be lucky if he rises above wiping up latrines in the air force."

Frederick kicked me in the face. Lying on the floor as I was, I had an interesting angle on the approach of the foot. He had on black leather boots. It must have been a style preference from the future. The toe of the boot caught me square in the right cheek. This time there was no question of something breaking. The bone in my cheek shattered. My head was jerked cruelly to the left where it smacked the wall. The motel room receded to a blurry red distance. Blood poured over my face. I felt Frederick grab me and shake me roughly.

"She was mine, you son of a bitch!" he swore. "You had no right to her."

I tried to smile. I could feel the teeth falling out of my mouth. "She told me you were afraid of the dark."

He shook me harder. "Where are they?"

"She said you sleep with a pink night-light on."

He pulled out his switchblade and held it to my throat. "Tell me where they are this second or I'll slit your windpipe!"

I swallowed thickly, feeling the touch of the cold blade through the stream of warm blood that poured down my neck. I could see the situation was already hopeless. The only reason he hadn't killed Vincent so far was that he wanted information about Becky and me. It may have had something to do with being in another person's body, but I felt no fear of Frederick. Vincent might have been with me more than I knew. All that was transpiring seemed inevitable.

"Tell me where we are first, and then I'll tell you where they are," I muttered.

A look of comprehension crossed his face. He threw me back against the wall. "They're trying to get to me through you!" he cried.

"Fair's fair," I whispered.

Frederick began to pace the room again. Even with my thoughts spinning, I saw something about his personality that should have immediately disqualified him from commanding a nuclear-armed space station: He was a goddamn lunatic.

"She doesn't care what she does to me!" he yelled. "She hates me. And what did I ever do to her? I'll tell you what. I saved her life. I had to drag her up to the station. And did she thank me? No! All she did was whine about what a temper I have. Temper! I'll show you temper. I'll kill all those bastards. I'll make them burn. I'll kill her!"

Frederick suddenly reached for me again, grabbing me by my messy shirt and hauling me to my feet, his knife held hard and tight in his other hand.

"Tell me where that bitch is right now before I stick this through your skin!" he yelled.

I forced another smile. I could feel Vincent coming near, like the rolling approach of rain from a distance. But before he could reach me and become one with me, I had to get in my last dig.

"She said you were lousy in bed," I muttered.

Frederick slit my throat. He dropped me to the floor like a soggy bag of potatoes and kicked me in the side with his boot. Then he wiped off his blade on his pants and stormed out of the motel room. I gulped in a thin breath and swallowed red fluid.

I began to die.

But first I had a life to live. Things to remember that were yet to be. Of course it was only through Vincent that I could recall what I had done with the next ten years of my life. He was with me now in full. I felt his presence in my soul like the soft chant of the words: "There is no fear where there is no second."

Truly I felt as one with him. I was not afraid. I began to remember living the life I would have lived if Vincent and Kara hadn't come back in time.

I was standing in the record store. I had just said goodbye to Becky. Just before I opened the door to leave, I thought I saw a young man standing in the software section with one of my games in his hand. I turned to get a better look. But there was no one there. I wondered if I was beginning to see things. I stepped outside, into the dark.

Home in my apartment, I worked on my next game. But during the night, when I was in bed, a horrible pain filled my chest. I got so scared I called the hospital. They told me to come in immediately, but then I got even more scared and decided to stay in bed. I thought of my mother and father. I thought of Becky. Eventually the pain in my chest subsided and I was able to sleep. I dreamed.

I dreamed I had the best friends in the world. A

guy and a girl, both of whom had blond hair that shone in the sun like gold. We would do everything together: go for walks, look at the stars, eat ice cream. The girl always ate chocolate ice cream, like Becky. It was the best dream I ever had, and when I woke up I was sad that it was over. But my chest felt better, and my life went on.

At least my life went forward. I saw Becky less and less often. She had a boyfriend. I didn't want to bother her. I tried to concentrate on my work, and in my self-imposed isolation, I developed my skills beyond what I had imagined possible. I began to write the most incredible computer games, with graphics and plots that few could match. Half my plots were taken from my dreams, from the conversations I continued to have with my two nightly visitors. They would tell me stories and I'd listen. They didn't come every night to me, but whenever they did, it hurt to say goodbye.

Becky quit her job at the record store. We talked a few times on the phone after that, but then I heard she was getting married. I didn't call her anymore. It didn't upset me that she didn't tell me about her marriage. I understood. She didn't want to hurt my feelings. She knew how I felt about her. Later, though, even when she was married and moved out of the area, I was tempted to try to find her again. I could never get her out of my mind.

I grew old, not in years, but physically. My health began to fail. I was rich from my computer games, but none of the specialists I saw could help me. I knew I was going to die young.

I bought a house in the hills that overlooked the

area where I had grown up. The house reminded me of the two friends who visited me in my dreams. But even they began to visit my dreams less and less often, and after my twenty-ninth birthday, they came no more. I felt truly alone. But I did not forget them or the stories they told me. I began to collect what they had said in a book. There was a cave in the hills not far from where I lived. It was there that I wrote most of the book, especially at night, when the moon was bright in the sky.

I was outside the cave entrance when my heart gave out.

The pain started in my chest, as it always did, like a dull weight that grew steadily in intensity until breathing was a strain. This time, however, sitting perfectly still and taking long gentle breaths did not ease the pain. It just kept growing. Soon I could barely move.

There was a gas lantern beside my notebook on a fold-out table. The table stood not far outside the entrance to the cave, on a dirt path that wound up into the hills. It was by the flame of the lantern that I had done the bulk of my work. My eyes automatically fixed on the flame as the breath inside me choked. I couldn't exhale. I could not bring in fresh oxygen. My body shook with minute convulsions. But the flame remained steady. It was protected by the glass cover of the lantern. It was safe from the wind, I thought, but what about the world? I believed much of the story I was writing, the tale the two golden-haired friends had told me in my dreams. I knew the winds of change were going to bring bad times for the earth. My main purpose in writing the story was to warn the world. But now, as my death approached, I felt that my story was incomplete. It was without hope. Everybody died. Suddenly I didn't want anyone to find the story after I was gone and think that I had died without hope.

I needed to destroy my story.

Gasping in air that could no longer feed my blood-starved heart, I reached out and managed to topple the gas lantern onto my notebook. The fuel in the container at the bottom of the lamp spilled out. Quickly it was ignited by the flame, and soon tall orange flames were licking across the tabletop and turning back the pages of my story, turning to the last pages and leaving them in ash. The flames leapt from the table and into the dry grass. The whole hilltop, I realized, would go up in smoke—the bushes and trees would be consumed. I don't know why, but I smiled then. Perhaps it was because I understood that now others would be able to find the cave. It had always been a special place to me. Or maybe I smiled because I knew that no one would find my body. I would become ash like the pages of my story.

I fell from my seat, onto the ground, rolling over on my back and staring up at the moon. It was so bright to me then, as bright as the midday sun, although its light was cool and soothing. Red flames began to dance around it.

They were hardly any different from the red blood that poured out of my cut throat.

Suddenly I was in two places at once: a cheap motel room and a burning hilltop. I was two people: Vincent and Mark. But we were soon to be one. The only thing that separated us now was that while Vincent was already in the light, I was just beginning to move toward it.

The flames touched the sleeve of my shirt. My heart gave a final agonizing squeeze and stopped. My head rolled on the motel floor. My lungs took a final gulp of my blood and were smothered. It didn't matter. I had no fear. I kept my eyes fixed on the moon. I could see it in the motel ceiling as well as in the night sky above the burning hilltop. I began to rush toward it with incredible speed. The moon, the white light. How obvious it was to me then that the Illumni should have appeared to come out of the moon. That they had come to Kara on a blissful wave of light.

Kara—I remembered her then. Just as I was about to drown in the white light, I remembered her and I saw the space station.

CHAPTER THIRTEEN

"Mark," Kara was saying. "Wake up. It's late. You have to come back. Mark, it's Kara. Can you hear me?"

I opened my eyes. The small flame of the lantern shone before me. Shadows stood patiently behind us on the cave walls. Our shadows, waiting for us to make a move. My eyes were damp.

"Did you reach him?" Kara asked.

"Yes," I whispered.

"Do you know where he is?"

"Yes."

"Where?"

I faced her, and in doing so I caught a glimpse of the cave opening. It was dark outside. The whole day had gone by and Kara had stayed by my side.

"He's with the Illumni," I said.

"What?"

"Frederick slit his throat. He's dead."

Frederick could have put the knife into her. Kara sucked in a breath and did not let it go. The light in her eyes went out. It was as if the shock had momentarily driven her soul from her body. Then her face crumpled and her head dropped to her chest. I put my arm around her. For a long time we sat there, making no sound at all. I didn't have to try to blank out my thoughts. My mind was empty.

Finally Kara stirred. She stood and walked to the far side of the chamber, where the cave continued through a narrow dark hole. Kneeling by the opening, she stared into it, at what I didn't know. When she finally spoke, the tone of her voice made me shiver. It was flat and cold.

"Frederick could do nothing if he didn't exist," she said.

"It's done," I said. "Another murder will help nobody."

She glanced over her shoulder. In the yellow light from the lamp, the lines of grief on her face were sharp and deep. She looked wicked.

"You forget the advantages of causality," she said.

"The Illumni didn't send you back in time to kill."

"They didn't send me here to fail either!" she snapped, jumping up. "He has to be stopped. He'll kill Becky. He'll kill you."

"You don't have time to find him. Vincent was in some motel room—I don't know where it was."

"You know I'm not talking about Frederick," she said.

I realized in a rush what she meant to do. "Kara,"

I pleaded. "Listen to yourself. He's a twenty-year-old boy. He hasn't done anything wrong."

"You don't know him!" she yelled. "He killed millions. In the war, when it was over, he kept shooting off our missiles. He used them all up, on small villages even, where the people's only crime was that they were born on the wrong side of the lines on his map. He has to be stopped."

"He didn't start the war, Kara."

"He didn't stop it either!"

"And you think you will by killing Ray?"

She put her hands to her face. She lowered her voice. "I cannot leave without Vincent. I told you that."

"He's gone." I stood. "But I'm here. I'll stay with you. We'll stay in this cave. Vincent would tell you the same thing. Don't do it, Kara."

She took her hands down from her face. She gripped her right wrist with her left hand. It was shaking and she couldn't stop it, just as I wasn't going to be able to stop her.

"I loved him more than the moon," she said miserably. She dropped her hands to her sides and took a step toward the cave entrance. "Good-bye, Mark. Maybe I'll see you later."

I tried to grab her as she hurried by, but I was weak from my lengthy trance. She pushed me away, and I hit my head on the wall of the cave and fell. The shadows jumped. I looked on in disbelief. Even though Kara was gone, there were still two shadows. Waiting.

*　　*　　*

Kara must have broken into a dead sprint the moment she stepped onto the path outside the cave. By the time I reached it there was no sign of her. I knew it was hopeless to try to catch her. The moon had just risen, and its light was bright on the hill. I wondered how much time she had left. I struggled down the path as best I could. Less than halfway to the house, I heard the start of a car engine, the burn of peeling rubber. Maybe a cop would stop her and give her a ticket, I hoped.

That morning we had driven Kara's car to the record store and the bookstore. Vincent's black Ferrari was at my apartment. I was stranded without wheels. Sitting in the kitchen where we had found the heart, I considered my options. I could call the police. I was sure I could think up some story to convince them that Kara was dangerous. But there were problems with the idea. In all probability, the police wouldn't be able to locate her right away. And I couldn't send them to guard Ray because I didn't know where Ray was, not for sure. Even if he was at the bookstore, I couldn't see the police putting a ring of armed men around him just because I asked them to. More than any of these things, however, I hated the idea of turning Kara over to the authorities. I didn't want her to be in jail when her end came.

Then there was the idea of calling the bookstore. I dismissed it almost immediately. Frederick had already spoken to Ray. Ray was already on his guard. If I gave him further warning, there was no telling what he'd do to Kara when she showed up.

In the end, I called Becky. It seemed logical. I had

no illusions about trying to get Becky to enter Kara's mind. Ray would be dead by the time I could explain the whole story, never mind the fact that Becky wouldn't believe a word of it. But I thought Becky, being Kara, would know what Kara would do next. Whispering a prayer that she wouldn't hang up on me, I dialed Becky's number.

"Hello?" Becky said, the first ring hardly over.

"Becky, it's Mark. Ray's in danger."

There was a long pause. "What do you want?" she asked.

"Remember that girl who came into your store? The one who went out with Ray?"

"Yeah. What about her?"

"It's a long story, but you've got to help me. You've got to come to where I am."

"How is Ray in danger?"

I had to move carefully. If I gave her too much information, she would call Ray. She might call him anyway, I thought.

"Becky," I said. "Until this morning, you and I were good friends. Hate me tomorrow if you must, but for tonight, just for tonight, I'm asking you to trust me. Please?"

There was another pause. "Where are you?"

I gave her directions to the house. She told me to give her thirty minutes. Hanging up the phone, I wished to God she had a Ferrari.

It wasn't an easy half-hour to kill. The horror of Vincent's slit throat came back to haunt me. If I hadn't pushed Frederick, would Vincent still be alive? Useless questions to ask, I realized, those that began with the word *if*. Except in a universe where the effects of causality could be overruled. My guilt remained, unsoothed by the beautiful white light I had beheld at the end of my trance. Kara was right. It was not something that could be imagined, or even properly remembered.

I went into Vincent's bedroom. I had left the computer on while Kara and I hiked up to the cave. I restarted the game, finally understanding why Vincent had given it the name he had—"Decision." But what had he wanted me to decide, I asked myself? Colored indicators on the screen flashed on and off, asking what weapon I wanted to fire first, what submarine or city I wanted to destroy. They were keyed to the number pad: one through ten. Then it hit me. The answer had been obvious from the beginning. I pushed the numeral zero. The space station vanished and was replaced by one word in big white letters: CONGRATULATIONS.

The only way to win the game was to not play.

Becky took forty minutes to reach the house. I was outside waiting for her by that time. I didn't even give her a chance to turn off the engine. I jumped in beside her. Her brown eyes looked at me with open concern.

"Where's Ray right now?" I asked.

"Why?"

"Just tell me."

She checked her watch. "It's nine-thirty. He's working tonight. I'm sure he's closing. He'll probably be there till ten."

"Drive me to the mall right now."

"What's going on?"

"Kara is upset with Ray. She might hurt him."

"Kara," she muttered. "Who's Kara?"

"That girl who went out with Ray. Let's go. Now!"

Becky backed out of the driveway. She was *not* a fast driver. She must have picked up the habit later, in a car of the future that did a cool three hundred miles an hour, or in a marriage that drove her to live dangerously. I implored her to use greater speed.

"Becky," I said as we drove down the hill and into the city. "I have to ask you a strange question."

"What's gotten into you, Mark?"

"Believe me, it's been a weird few days. I want you to think before you answer my question. If you were mad at Ray, so mad you wanted to kill him—how would you do it?"

"Mark!"

"Please, I need to know."

"Why? You're not going to hurt Ray, are you? It's over between us, thanks to you. Haven't you hurt us enough?"

"I told you," I said, trying to keep my voice calm, "it's Kara who will hurt Ray. You have to tell me how she will do it."

"Have you lost your mind?"

I paused. "Yes. I think I may have lost it."

We lapsed into a strained silence. Becky was finally picking it up, running a red light and cruising through a stop sign. I let her concentrate on her driving. I was lost in my own pain. From the time I got out of bed that morning, it was impossible to imagine how I could have screwed up worse. I had lost my girlfriend, been beaten up, gotten killed, and driven my future wife to murder. I didn't know which was the greater sin. Each act seemed a part of the same big monster. I knew what Vincent would have said: it was meant to be. But Vincent was dead. I couldn't hear him anymore. Since I had come out of my trance, I couldn't even *feel* him inside me. It was as if I had left the better part of myself in the light when I stepped back into the world.

I felt Becky's hand on my knee.

"Are you all right?" she asked.

"No."

"What's wrong?"

"I'm dying," I said, feeling sorry for myself.

Her face wrinkled in anxiety. "Are you sick?"

"Yes."

"What's wrong?" she asked.

I shrugged. "What's right? You hate me. You and Ray hate each other. Kara hates Ray. Ray probably hates Kara."

"I don't hate you, Mark."

"You certainly don't love me," I said.

Becky took back her hand. She ran another red light, this time without looking both ways. She seemed to be thinking.

"Can you tell me why you did it?" she asked finally.

"I didn't do it," I said. "But I let it be done."

"Didn't you realize how much it would hurt me? Didn't you care?"

"I care. I think that's why I let Kara go ahead with her plan."

"Who is this Kara?"

"She's just a girl I know," I said.

"Why did you say you're dying?"

"I have a bad heart. I've had it since I was a child."

"Why didn't you tell me?" she asked.

"I didn't want you to feel sorry for me."

"You still should have told me."

"Why would you care?" I asked, suddenly tired of being Mr. Nice Guy. "The only time you were interested in going out with me was when your boyfriend was unfaithful. Some girl you are. You really know how to pick them. You know what Ray's goal is? To become president of the United States so he can blow up China from outer space."

"Who told you he wants to be president?" she asked, surprised.

"You don't even like the way I dress."

"How do you know all this?"

I stopped. "You really don't like my clothes?"

"They're OK. But sometimes you look as if—"

"My mother dresses me," I interrupted.

Becky frowned. "How did you know I was going to say that?"

"Kara told me you would."

"Who is this girl?" she asked for what seemed like the tenth time.

"Tell me your first name and I'll tell you who she is."

Becky hesitated. "It's Kara."

I looked at her. "You only tell those you really love your first name," I said.

She was amazed. "How did you know that?"

"Did you want to tell it to me?" I asked.

Becky stopped at a red light. There were no cars coming in either direction. Kara was probably adjusting the telescopic sight on her rifle. The bookstore had been closed awhile. Still, I didn't hurry Becky. She bit her lower lip.

"Last night," she said. "I told you my first name while you were asleep. I didn't think you heard me."

"I didn't."

She reached over and put her hand on the back of my neck. "But you knew my name before I told you," she said. "How?"

I looked out the window. The moon continued to rise in the black sky. "I dreamed it," I said.

"I'm sorry."

"What are you sorry about?"

Becky leaned over and kissed me. "I just feel sorry, that's all. About everything, I guess. I wish you didn't have a bad heart."

"So do I." I held her tight for a moment before letting go. "We have to hurry."

CHAPTER FOURTEEN

The parking lot at the mall was all but deserted. There were only three cars visible. One of them was Ray's red BMW. I could see no sign of a red Ferrari. I wondered if Kara was already inside the store blowing away her old boyfriend. Becky interrupted my thoughts.

"I would just run him over," she said.

"What?" I asked.

"You asked me how I would kill Ray. I'd just run him over as he walked to his car."

I studied where Ray had parked his BMW. He probably didn't want people opening car doors into it. It was about a hundred and fifty yards of open asphalt from the back door of the bookstore. I estimated that distance would take him twenty seconds to cover at a full sprint. I reminded myself that Kara's car could accelerate at g-force.

"Are you sure?" I asked.

"The other day, when I learned he had gone out with another girl, I spent an hour fantasizing exactly how I would do it, where I would park and stuff."

"Where would you park?"

Becky pointed to the far side of the mall, over a quarter of a mile away and poorly lit. "On the other side of Mervyn's department store. You see how the corner of the store is all windows? If you parked beyond those windows, you could see Ray when he came out."

I squinted my eyes. I could see the windows, but not if there was a car on the other side of them. I considered having Becky swing around the store, but then decided it would be better if Kara was unaware of us. I had this thought of first letting Kara come out into the open before pouncing. I think I had seen too many cop movies. Becky was watching me.

"This girl's not really going to try to kill Ray, is she?" she asked.

"It's a possibility. That's all I can say." I gestured to the back of the mall. "Let's put your car behind that dumpster over there. I want to get out and walk."

Becky did as I requested. Once out and up on our feet, I began to check around for a secret way into the mall. Like I would find one just because I needed it. Right. Becky figured out what I was trying to do.

"Why don't we just go knock at the security door?" she asked. "The guards all know me. I used to come by to see Ray after hours all the time."

I agreed to the idea. I still wasn't sure what I was trying to do, but I thought if we could get to the other side of the parking lot via the inside of the mall, then we could hide out where neither Ray nor Kara could see us, and make sure they didn't kill each other. If we just walked across the parking lot, I knew Kara would see us.

Becky had to pound on the security door to get someone's attention. One look at the guy who finally answered the door told us why. He was a couple of years older than we were, and dressed in a uniform, but his pupils were as big as the moon in the sky. He reeked of marijuana smoke. His grin took up most of his face.

"Becky!" he said. "Are you here or do I just think you are?"

Becky nodded. "I'm here, Ted. What are you up to?"

Ted waved his hand. Then stopped to make sure it hadn't fallen off the end of his arm. He burst into a laugh.

"Just killing clocks, babe. Got to put in the clocks to get paid."

"You mean, you're killing time," I said.

Ted shielded his eyes, as if the mere sight of me dazzled him as much as the sun. "Hey, who is this guy? Is he really here?"

"No," Becky said. "But could you let us in? We have to talk to Ray. It's important."

"Sure," Ted said, letting us go by. "Just don't steal anything. I'll have to pay for it."

We left Ted sitting in front of his four security TV screens. He had *E.T.* running on all of them. Walking through the center of the mall with no one around was spooky. I asked Becky to take off her leather-heeled shoes. The slightest sound echoed the length of the mall. Ray's bookstore was on the ground level, not too far from the Mervyn's Becky had referred to.

"I don't want Ray to see us," I said to Becky. "Is there a store near the bookstore that we could go through to get to the parking lot?"

"The stores are all locked from the inside," Becky said, gesturing at the iron gates that covered all the display windows. "But I doubt that Ted locked the hallways that lead to the bathrooms. The janitors clean the johns after hours."

"Where are they?"

"On the far side of the bookstore," Becky said.

"Great. We better go up to the second floor and come back down farther along. I don't want Ray spotting us sneaking past his store."

"Can't we just warn him that this girl is dangerous?"

"No," I said.

"Why not?"

I couldn't very well tell her that Ray was even more dangerous than Kara. Especially when I didn't know if it was true. But I was worried about Frederick. Where had he gone after slitting Vincent's throat? To talk to Ray? How much time did Frederick have left? A day? A month? There was so much I didn't know.

"That would just make things worse," I said. "Trust me."

Becky smiled at me. "I trust you, Mark."

I got her drift. "This is not like my game," I said quickly.

"You mean I'm not the queen of the universe?"

"Ask me later," I said, not sure what I meant.

We ran up a flight of stairs and down one on the far side of the bookstore. I hoped Ray was still at work in the back.

As Becky predicted, the door leading to the bathrooms on the first floor was unlocked. The rest rooms were at the far end of a long, drab hallway. Beyond them was an emergency exit. Just our luck, I thought. We couldn't open the door without everyone knowing it. We'd probably even bring Ted running.

We hurried to the end of the hall. Two wires—one red, the other blue—were attached to the hinge of the door. I checked my watch. It was ten after ten. The time for subtlety was past. I ripped the wires out. Becky jumped, but no alarm went off. Holding my breath, I cracked the door an inch and peered outside. Ray's BMW was still there.

"He hasn't left," I said.

"That's weird," Becky said, sounding far away.

Preoccupied, I hadn't noticed the change in her voice. I shifted my angle. Now we were too close to the wall of Mervyn's to see through the corner windows Becky had pointed out. Mervyn's was to our right, the bookstore to our left. I pulled back from the door. It was only then I noticed that Becky had slumped to the floor and was sitting with her eyes half-closed. Her last comment had not been in response to mine, I realized.

"What's wrong?" I asked, kneeling beside her. She rubbed her eyes with her hands, blinking.

"I just had the strangest feeling."

"What?"

"I can't describe it."

"Did you feel split in two?" I asked.

"Yes. Sort of."

"Close your eyes, Becky, quickly. Tell me what you see inside your head. Where are you?"

Becky didn't question my order. It was almost as if she had no choice in the matter. She was being sucked inside in the same way I had been when I fell down the long tunnel into the cheap motel room. She sat silent for several seconds. Her breathing deepened. Slowly her confused expression turned to one of contentment.

"I'm in a forest," she said, her voice soft and dreamy. "I'm with you and we're happy. The trees are pretty. They're all different colors."

She was talking about the Illumni's slice of paradise, I realized. Kara must be reminiscing about her time with Vincent. I considered having her open her eyes to see if there was a parking lot on the other side of the trees, but I was afraid it would take her out of Kara's mind.

"What are we doing?" I asked.

"We're talking, but we're not moving our lips. You can read my mind."

"Can you read mine?"

"No. It's not necessary. You look different."

"Do I have blond hair?" I asked.

"No. You're glowing."

"What?"

"You're lit up like a light bulb," Becky said.

"Are you?"

"No. But I'm happy."

"What are we discussing?" I asked.

"I don't know. I don't understand it. But it's nice."

"Is Ray there?"

"No. He's dead. I wish he was . . ." Becky's voice trailed off. For a moment she appeared confused; then a look of realization crossed her face. The problem was, I wasn't sure if it was Kara's realization or Becky's. Faintly, I heard the sound of a door open and close to our left. Becky suddenly leapt to her feet.

"No!" she shouted, her eyes flying wide open.

"What is it?" I asked, grabbing her arms.

"We have to stop him!"

"You mean Kara? We have to stop Kara? Is she here?"

Becky shook her head as if she were trying to shake out of it. "I don't want him to die," she cried.

"Who?"

"Please stop it!"

"Becky, who's going to die?"

"No! I can't tell you. You're not real."

Before I could respond, many things happened at once. But even before that, I had the crazy idea that Ted the security guard must also be from the future.

You're not real?

What did that mean?

I knew the door opening and closing outside must have been Ray leaving his bookstore. I didn't respond to it immediately because I still didn't know for sure if Kara was in the area. Or Frederick, for that matter. Plus I had to deal with Becky. Above all else, I knew I had to protect Becky. But that's the trouble with having a number-one priority. You strain so hard to accomplish it, it gets away from you. Becky struggled free of my grasp and ran out the door.

"Becky!" I called after her.

She had a jump on me and she was fast. By the time I got through the door, Becky was already a dozen feet into the wide-open parking lot. Ray was off to her left.

He was also farther away than Becky from the headlights that suddenly ripped around the corner of Mervyn's department store. They were aimed straight for him.

It was **Kara**'s red Ferrari.

When Ray saw the headlights barreling down on him, he froze. It was only for a moment, but Kara was sparing her clutch nothing. The rev of the engine vibrated across the entire lot. The car was coming at him like a missile launched from Vincent's space station. By the time Ray could get himself moving, the Ferrari was probably up to sixty miles an hour—and it was accelerating. Ray glanced at the door he had just exited, then at his car; back and forth his eyes darted. I thought his choice was clear. He had to head for the door to the bookstore. It was closer. But he chose his car instead. As he ran toward it, there was no question he realized the seriousness of his situation. I never saw a guy move so fast.

Unfortunately, a shopping cart got in his way. It was ironic. There wasn't even a supermarket at the mall. The nearest one was around the block. Probably some shopper from the space station had brought it over because they hadn't liked Ray either. They probably wanted to see what he would look like as a kid with a couple of retreads burned over the back of his skull. The shopping cart was one of those silver metal kind, but it was practically invisible in the dark. Ray hit it with a bang and down he went, the headlights of the Ferrari shining in his eyes like twin lasers locked on target and itching to be fired.

His sudden fall threw Kara off as well, though. The headlights might have flashed bright in Ray's eyes, but then they swept to his right, more in the direction of the mall. Kara was an excellent high-speed driver, but she had overcompensated for Ray's tripping. At the speed she was going, it was understandable. The Ferrari was easily up to eighty by now. Even though the parking lot was big, the car was out of control.

Then there was Becky. In all the excitement, I had momentarily forgotten about my number-one priority. I had forgotten to tell her when I called from Kara and Vincent's house that she should wear bright clothing. Becky had on black jeans and a black cotton sweater. She made the shopping cart look like a neon sign. Kara probably didn't have the slightest idea her other self was there, in spite of the fact that they had just mind-melded. Certainly she was so many years removed from the days when she loved Ray that Kara couldn't imagine that Becky would suddenly bolt in the direction of her fallen boyfriend—that Becky would risk her life to save Ray's.

"Becky!" I cried. I didn't freeze as Ray had. I was up on my toes in an instant and running. I was pretty fast, too, for a heart patient. I almost caught her. But she had that goddamn head start and I didn't have on my goddamn running shoes. The goddamn car was coming so goddamn fast. I almost saved her. For a second, as the roar of the engine and the glare of the headlights drowned out all else, I saw her in my mind's eye crying helplessly on top of the oil well. I had saved her then, I thought. Why couldn't I save her now? All I had to do was reach out and pull her to safety. The car would pass and the world would survive. It seemed so simple. But I think that is how it is with all miracles in life, and all tragedies. They are so simple they can't be comprehended, even as they transpire before your eyes.

"Becky!" I cried as I leapt for a handful of her sweater. I leapt as far as I could, with every bit of strength in my body. But I had been born weak. I missed. I landed face first on a hard ground, which scraped the skin from the end of my nose. White lights swam over my head, harsh and blinding. A squeal as from a tortured animal rent the night. Kara had slammed on her brakes and the hard ground was now scraping away melting rubber. Too late, and not enough.

I heard a cry. A human cry. My love. I heard the two of them scream in unison. Then there was a horrible thud followed by an even more horrible silence. I tried burying myself in the hard ground, but it would not have me. I suppose it was against the rules to die twice in the same day. I had to get up and live. I staggered to my feet.

The Ferrari had hit Becky. Of that there was no doubt. She lay crumpled in a heap no less than thirty feet from the glaring headlights of the now stationary car. The force of the impact must have thrown her through the air. There was blood on the ground near her head, a small puddle not much different from the color of the black asphalt. I tried not to see it. I looked at Kara instead. She stood just outside the open door of her Ferrari, her fingers in her mouth. I wanted to tell her to turn off the blasted headlights. They were beginning to hurt my eyes. I wanted to tell her that she shouldn't have pushed so hard for everything to work out.

"Kara," Kara said. It didn't sound funny. I watched as Kara walked slowly toward herself. I was watching again, I was not acting. I was never going to learn. But those goddamn headlights. I couldn't see a thing beyond the glare of them.

Kara knelt in the light and took Becky's head in her hands. I wanted to tell her that she shouldn't move her, that Becky might have a spinal injury. But then I figured Kara would know exactly what bones Becky had broken and how long it would be before the moon rose too far into the sky. The dark puddle beside Becky's head continued to grow. My feet began to take me toward them, one step at a time.

"This was not supposed to be," Kara told Becky, her voice gentle and forgiving. It was confusing to hear forgiveness in her voice instead of apology. But then it made perfect sense.

Ray stepped into the tunnel of light cut by the car's high beams.

He had a gun in his hand.

"Kara!" I screamed.

Ray pointed his weapon in Kara's direction.

"Don't move!" he ordered me as I attempted to place myself between them. I stopped cold. Fury had twisted Ray's face beyond recognition. For an instant I wasn't even sure it was Ray. It could have been Frederick. But the doubt only lasted until he spoke again. He gestured to Kara with the barrel of the revolver, which Frederick had no doubt given him. "Who are you?" he demanded.

Kara carefully eased Becky's head onto the pavement. She stood and faced Ray. There was blood on her hands. Perhaps she should have held them up for Ray to see. Perhaps he would have taken pity on her if he had been told it was her blood. But I should have known she'd ask no pity from him.

"I am nobody now," she said.

Ray shook his gun. "You bitch!"

Kara sighed. Then she drew in a deep breath and looked at the sky. Not at the moon, but at the few stars that were visible. And it seemed to me that she was remembering all the times, throughout the long course of their unhappy marriage, that he had called her a bitch. Finally she lowered her head and stared him straight in the eye.

"You bastard," she said.

Ray shot her in the chest. Kara dropped to the ground.

The chase by the Ferrari and the confrontation with Kara appeared to have left Ray a bit dazed. I had to get to him before he could turn the gun in my direction. I'm not sure if he would have tried to shoot me if I hadn't attacked him. But now that I was jumping him, I was the enemy. I had to be destroyed. I leapt onto his right side, both my arms wrapped around his neck. I probably should have played football. It was a hell of a tackle. Ray went down with me riding on top of him.

"Son of a bitch!" he swore as the side of his head hit the pavement. Pleased with the effect the blow had on his personality, I let go of his neck and grabbed his hair near his right temple and slammed his head into the pavement again. Ray's grip on his gun loosened. It fell out of his hand onto the pavement. I immediately reached for it. I was in too much of a hurry and succeeded only in knocking it out of my reach.

"Dammit," I said. Ray appeared to be only semiconscious. I decided it was worth the risk to jump off him to get to the gun. I almost made it. But he was not that unconscious. He grabbed my ankle and hauled me back just as my fingertips were brushing against the barrel. It really pissed me off. I reacted instinctively. I kicked him in the face several times. He finally let go of my foot and I made another lunge for the gun. This time I got it. Pivoting on my knees, I raised it in his direction, directly into the glare of the lights.

"Hold it right there!" I ordered.

Either Ray thought he was Superman or else he had already started his dive before I could tell him to stop. He crashed into me with the force of a freight train. This time it was my head that hit the pavement. A dark purple light swelled inside my brain. I saw stars. I saw galaxies. But I didn't let go of the gun. Feeling Ray clawing at my hand for it, I swung my right knee into his crotch. He was tougher than I thought. These ex-jocks—he probably wore a cup even in the bookstore. He just grunted and kept trying to grab the gun. The weight of his body on my chest was suffocating. He was wriggling my finger away from the trigger. I was losing the fight.

Suddenly the gun went off. One of the Ferrari headlights exploded in a crash of glass and went out. Then there was another shot. This one didn't appear to hit anything. It also sounded different. It wasn't until I heard Ted the security guard shout out that I understood the second shot had come from another gun.

"Hold it right there!" he ordered Ray.

"Go to hell!" Ray swore.

Ted put his revolver to Ray's head and pulled back the hammer. "What did you say, buddy?" Ted asked.

Ray stopped fighting with me. Slowly he turned his head to look at Ted's loaded gun. "All right," he said in resignation.

Ted had the two of us get up. He had sobered up some since we last saw him, but he still had a long way to go. He made both of us put our hands above our heads. His eyes kept straying uneasily to Kara and Becky. Kara had fallen beside her younger counterpart. She was bleeding freely from a chest wound. Neither girl was moving.

"What's going on here?" Ted cried.

"That girl ran over Becky," Ray said bitterly.

"This bastard shot Kara," I said, lowering my arms.

"Don't call me a bastard," Ray yelled, also taking down his hands, and balling them into fists.

"Shut up, both of you," Ted said, moving close to

182

Becky. Keeping his gun pointed at us, he knelt beside her and felt for a pulse at her neck. He had tears on his face. He moaned. "We've got to get Becky to the hospital."

I turned to Ray. "You take Becky. I'll take Kara."

"Who's that girl?" he demanded, pointing to Kara. I noticed Ray didn't react to the sameness of names. Becky must not have told him her first name yet. His question was interesting in another respect. He had gone out with Kara, yet he was asking about her as if he was missing something, which of course he was.

"It's Becky's twin," I said.

"Becky doesn't have a twin," Ray growled.

"Look at her!" I said. "They're identical."

Ted allowed Ray to step to where he was standing over Kara. It was as if Ray was seeing her for the first time. I could relate to that. Kara had been right about its being impossible to recognize what you think is impossible.

"Jesus Christ," Ray whispered, his face white in the glare from the remaining headlight. Ted almost dropped his gun when he saw the similarity. I used the opportunity to move to Kara's side. She lay on her back, her eyes closed, her breathing ragged. I touched her cheek. It was as cold as marble.

"Kara," I said. "Can you hear me?"

"Yes," she whispered.

"What should I do?"

She coughed weakly. Her eyes remained closed. "Take me home."

"Where's that? Kara? Kara?" She lapsed into unconsciousness. I pressed my hand on the messy hole beneath her right breast. Sticky warmth spread around my fingers. The bleeding was not going to be stopped without an operation, if it could be stopped at all. Yet the fact she was alive at all meant an artery couldn't have been hit. I looked up at the others. "We're running out of time," I said.

"We should wait for the ambulance," Ted said.

"Did you call an ambulance?" Ray asked.

Ted thought a moment. "No, I forgot."

Ray nodded to me. "OK. You take Kara. I'll take Becky. Do you know where the nearest hospital is?"

"Yes," I said.

Ray knelt and carefully lifted Becky from the ground. She hung in his powerful arms like a broken doll, her long dark hair sticky with clots of blood.

"I'll meet you there," Ray said.

"Yes," I repeated. I watched him put Becky in the backseat of his car. I watched Ted climb into the front seat. I watched them drive away before realizing that the hospital was not the place for me to go. I remembered a remark Kara had made about the Illumni's time machine.

"We never actually saw it before we left, although we felt it at work. I suppose it could be there even now. The inside of the cave does have a timeless quality about it."

Causality. It had been both Kara's friend and her enemy. The Illumni had given her a chance to change her future, but in another sense they had taken away her place in the future. There could not be two of them, she had said. It made sense. It also made sense that if Becky died, Kara would cease to exist in all

184

possible futures. I didn't like the odds. Becky's head wound was grievous. I had little faith in what the doctors could do for her. But Kara, I thought, stood more of a chance to survive.

A timeless quality?

I wondered if the laws of causality applied inside the cave. And if Kara was inside when Becky died—if Becky died—if time's hourglass would not turn over one more time, and leave Kara alone. It was an interesting question. It could be both girls' only hope.

I lifted Kara into the backseat of the Ferrari. Her blood soaked the front of my shirt. She clasped my hand as I strapped her in.

"What time is it?" she asked.

"It's still early," I said.

CHAPTER FIFTEEN

My heart had so far withstood the stress of the evening's events, but there was no way I was going to be able to carry Kara the three-quarters of a mile from the house to the cave. It was all uphill. Necessity is the mother of invention. In this case it was also the ruin of a fairly expensive paint job. When I got to the house, I kept right on driving. A knee-high wooden fence was all that separated the yard from the hills and the start of the path. It was the first thing to fall to the bumper of the Ferrari. The boards cracked beneath the wheels, and Kara moaned in the backseat.

"Hang on," I said. "We're almost there."

The path wound dangerously and was mostly made up of loose dirt. Traction was a problem. My main concern, however, was the width of the path. There simply wasn't enough space to accommodate the car.

I had to make the space. Many bushes paid. They tore at the sides of the Ferrari as I ground them into the dust. A couple of young trees didn't go down so easily. I had to floor the accelerator and ram them. We were lucky I didn't drive off the edge.

Vincent's telescope was standing in the center of the path. I almost knocked it down as well. I guessed that Frederick hadn't given Vincent time to put it away. I didn't stop to think that Vincent would never have had the telescope out in the daytime, when he had in all probability been kidnapped.

Ray's bullet had not gone all the way through Kara. There was no bloodstain on her back. Not knowing the type of bullet in Ray's gun, I didn't know if that was a good thing. Her blood was all over the backseat, but she was still conscious. She peered out the window.

"What are we doing here?" she asked weakly.

"I've brought you home," I said.

I hated to pick her up again. She tried not to let me know how painful the wound was, but I could see her clenching her teeth so she wouldn't scream.

"Don't drop me," she said.

"Never."

When I finally got her out of the car and was standing in the middle of the path with her arms draped loosely around my neck, I marveled at how light she felt. Perhaps I could have carried her all the way up the path. She felt as if she were made of space, and I gripped her hair to make sure she was not leaving me too soon. The moon was high in the sky and I stared at it anxiously.

187

"Not yet," I told it. "Give me a few minutes."

I carried her into the cave. The way was dark, but we reached the inner chamber quickly. The lantern was still lit. I assumed I had forgotten to blow it out. I laid Kara on a stone ledge and rolled a blanket beneath her head. It was cool—I wished there was a second blanket. I made another feeble attempt at putting pressure on her wound to stop the bleeding. She waved me away.

"It's too late for that," she whispered, her eyes shut, her cheeks damp with perspiration.

"You're not going to die," I said.

"Becky is going to die."

"You don't know that for sure."

She opened her eyes, smiled faintly. "I remember all the times you used to say that to me. You were wrong, you know." Her eyes strayed to our shadows on the walls. Her smile vanished. "But so was I."

"It wasn't your fault."

"From the very beginning, it was all my fault." She nodded, her eyes glazed and staring. "Becky will die soon."

"You're with her?"

"Yes."

"Is she at the hospital?" I asked.

"Yes. They're in emergency."

"Is Ray with her?"

"Yes," a voice said at my back.

Frederick came out of the black hole at the far end of the chamber. There were bloodstains on the leg of his pants. He had not changed since he cut Vincent's throat. He still had his knife. He held the blade out for us to see as he strode casually our way. Kara tried to sit up, but couldn't manage it.

"Don't push," I whispered to her.

"Now who do we have here?" Frederick asked, stopping a couple of feet away.

"My name's Mark Forum," I said.

Frederick nodded. "We've met, haven't we?"

"No," I said.

"Yes, we have," Frederick insisted. "You visited me in the motel room this afternoon. You said something about me being less than a man."

I shrugged. "You know how it is when you're in another body. Things don't always come out the way you mean them."

Frederick slowly smiled. "You're very funny."

"Thank you," I said.

Frederick slid his blade beneath my throat. "Entertain me."

"Fred," Kara said quickly.

"What?" he asked.

"You know what's happened?" she asked.

"Yes," he said.

"Then you know you've won," Kara said. "Becky's finished. I'm finished. Leave Mark alone."

Frederick shook his head. "No, I don't think so. Too risky. He might try to mess with Ray. I can't chance that."

"I promise I won't," I said. The knife against my Adam's apple didn't feel any better the second time

189

around. There were disadvantages to being in one's own body. I tried not to swallow. I was acting cool, but inside I was ready to pee in my pants. I could handle the sight of blood as long as it wasn't gushing out of my jugular. All of a sudden twenty-nine sounded like a ripe old age to me.

"And you expect me to believe you?" Frederick asked me.

"He expects you to do what you were trained to do," Kara said. "You're supposed to protect people."

Frederick was not impressed. But he did temporarily withdraw his knife from my throat. My eyes darted about the chamber for a possible weapon. I noticed a coil of rope sitting on the ledge across from us. I assumed Frederick had used a piece of it to tie up Vincent. I didn't imagine I'd get too far trying to whip Frederick to death with it. The only other thing was the lantern. I ran through an elaborate scenario in my mind whereby I threw the fuel in Frederick's face and set it on fire. All I needed was a Phillips screwdriver and five minutes of undisturbed work on the base of the lantern. I had no illusions about attacking Frederick directly. I figured I would last about three and a half seconds. Even though he looked exactly like Ray, I knew he was meaner and stronger. He regarded Kara critically.

"You're bleeding," he said.

"You shot me," she replied.

"Are you in pain?" he asked.

"No," she said.

He nodded. "You're in a lot of pain. But you're

only one person. This guy's only one person. You saw what kind of pain the country went through."

"The world went through," Kara corrected, shifting uneasily as a spasm went through her body that she couldn't hide. "You think killing Mark's going to stop the war?"

Frederick sneered. "Did you think killing Ray would stop it?"

"You're the one who attacked us," Kara said. "I was content to leave you alone."

"Does leaving me alone include stealing my girl?"

"I'm not your girl," Kara snapped. "I don't belong to you."

"Don't worry," Frederick said. "I don't want you."

"Then what do you want?" Kara asked. "Why did you come back in time? You've been with the Illumni. You must know force won't work. It can't save the world."

"The Illumni never told me that," Frederick said.

"You lie."

"They never said a word to me about nonviolence," Frederick said. "Just the opposite. They told me I had to be strong. That I had to make strong decisions if I was going to change things."

"Right," Kara said sarcastically. "Cutting a young man's throat is a sign of strength."

"He wasn't a young man!" Frederick shouted. "He was a stinking corpse. He'd been dead for thirty years. I just put him back in the ground where he belonged."

"Where you belong, you mean," Kara spat back.

There followed a much-needed silence. Frederick moved back a step and contemplated his shadow on the wall. Kara briefly closed her eyes. Lying down as she was—not to mention the fact that she was bleeding to death and that Frederick was carrying a switchblade—she should have been at a distinct psychological disadvantage in their argument. But she was holding her own, and I would have admired her for it if something hadn't begun to trouble me. Frederick was a maniac—there was no question about that. Yet Kara had a bit of him in her. Her solutions to problems had always been dramatic—one might even say violent. This was not to say she was in her nasty husband's league, but it was easy to imagine the two of them arguing for the next forty years . . . all over again.

"How is Becky?" I whispered.

"She'll go any second now," Kara whispered back, her eyes still closed. She arched her back slightly and sucked in a tight breath. The drops of perspiration on her face were as big as tears, and I had no handkerchief to wipe them away. She was speaking for the two of them.

"Are they going to operate on her?" I asked.

"The doctors have given up on her," she said.

I had expected as much; nevertheless, the words cut like blades. "Is she unconscious?" I asked.

"Yes."

"Is there any possibility of her regaining consciousness?"

"I don't think so," Kara said.

"Could you make her regain consciousness?" I asked.

Kara paused. "Maybe."

"Is Ray still with her?"

Kara opened her eyes and glared at her husband. He glared back at her. "Unfortunately," she said.

"It will do him good to watch her die," Frederick said. "It will make him strong."

The cruelty of the remark went beyond anything imaginable. It did not make sense that this man could have been the same man the president of the United States had put in charge of the most powerful military installation America had at its disposal. The war must have done this to Frederick, I thought. Seeing his country burn from outer space and being unable to stop it. Something must have snapped inside him. It was as if a demon peered out from behind his eyes.

Yet he must have been ready to snap. He must have been beaten before the war began. Throughout her description of her life, Kara had said he was always a demon, always at fault. The only one at fault in their marriage. I wasn't ready to defend him, but I did know from my brief experiences that there were always two sides to a story. Or maybe I knew it because Vincent had told me when we were together. For the first time since exiting my trance, I felt him close to me, like a warm feeling deep inside me. An idea that had been slowly forming in my head suddenly became crystal clear.

"May I make a suggestion?" I said.

"Can it," Frederick said. "You're history."

"Listen to Mark," Kara said. "He's smarter than both of us put together."

"I've been listening to you two," I said, watching Frederick for a sign of interest. "And something has occurred to me. You two don't like each other very much."

Frederick chuckled. "He's smart, all right."

Kara touched my hand. "What do you mean?"

"I mean," I said addressing them both, "that you've forgotten you once loved each other."

Kara looked sad. "I don't think I ever loved him."

Frederick chuckled again, although this time it was obviously forced. "Forget the amateur counseling, Forum. It ain't going to save your skin."

"I am worried about saving my skin," I admitted. "But I saw someone tonight who wasn't. It was Becky. You say you know what happened in the parking lot. I assume you were able to see through Ray's eyes. If that's true, then you must know that Becky leapt in front of the car in an effort to save you."

"It swerved and hit her accidentally," Frederick snapped back.

"Did it?" I asked Kara.

Kara hated to admit the truth. "No. It was no accident. She did try to save the bastard."

"Well, I'm touched," Frederick said bitterly, moving close again. "I'm really touched. Some dimwitted teenager jumps in front of a speeding car and I'm supposed to give up my plans to win the war this time."

194

"But you can't win the war," I said.

Frederick snorted. "Don't lecture me. If we had hit them hard at the beginning, they wouldn't have hit back. It's as simple as that."

I realized I wasn't going to win an argument with him concerning nuclear strategy. "Let's forget about the war for a minute," I said. "Your wife is lying here with a bullet inside her. Don't you feel anything?"

Frederick scowled at Kara. "She's not my wife."

"Oh, swell," Kara whispered. She was having trouble breathing.

"She is your wife," I told Frederick. "You married her when you were a young man. And right now that young man is with Becky in the hospital. Do you know how he feels?"

Frederick wanted to snap at me, but chose to say nothing instead. I was encouraged. I mean, we were talking about a guy who planned to slit my throat any minute. Something I said had touched a chord in him. Or maybe it was his watching Kara. He couldn't take his eyes off her. The flesh around his mouth quivered. Kara squeezed my hand.

"You don't know what we've been through together," she said, blood appearing at the corner of her mouth. She wiped it away and grimaced at the sight of it on the back of her hand. She added, "The wall between us is too thick."

"There are things neither of us will ever forget," Frederick agreed. "How do you feel?" he asked Kara.

"Weak," she whispered.

"It's your own fault," Frederick said.

"Thank you," Kara said.

"Ray and Becky have nothing to forget," I interrupted, afraid to let them get started again. "They haven't lived yet. Why don't you ask *them* what you should do."

"I know what to do, Forum," Frederick said. "I've done it. I just have to finish it."

"Do you really want to kill me?" I asked.

Frederick bristled. "It has nothing to do with what I want. It's what has to be. Ray has to be left to fulfill his destiny. He could go down in history as the greatest hero this world has known."

"Please," Kara said. "Spare us your visions of destiny." Yet she was interested in what I was proposing. "You want us to go into their minds?" she asked.

"Yes," I said.

"What for?" Kara asked.

"Your bodies have come back in time," I said. "But you're still locked in a horrible future. I think you've got to come all the way back."

Frederick snorted. "If you think I'm going to sit here and close my eyes while you run off to the police, you must be out of your mind."

I gestured to the rope on the other side of the chamber. "You tied me up once today and I didn't get away."

Frederick shook his head vigorously. "This is idiotic. Someone in your position telling me what to do. You should be on your knees praying that you die as painlessly as your twin."

I couldn't argue with him. I had no good reason why he should listen to me. All I could talk about was a fresh perspective, when he was obsessed with how many megatons he could float over the enemy. Kara spoke up.

"Perhaps we should do it," she said.

"No," Frederick said. "You're just trying to trap me."

Kara coughed up more blood. "What are you afraid of?"

Frederick was angry. "I'm not afraid of anything."

"I am," Kara said softly. "I'm afraid of dying. But I wonder if Becky is."

"Becky's in a coma," Frederick growled.

Kara raised an eyebrow. "You *are* there."

Frederick nodded reluctantly. "How could I help but be there?"

"Then let's go all the way," Kara said. "What have we got to lose?"

"What have I got to gain?" Frederick asked, and I think he was scared. I could understand. It was almost easier to die than to become someone you couldn't remember, or someone who had once been dead.

For the first time since Frederick had entered the chamber, Kara's expression softened. "You're going to have to face the end soon," she said. "It doesn't matter what you do to Mark. Or what Ray does."

"I've faced it before," Frederick said proudly.

Kara nodded. "It was hard."

"It was hard," Frederick agreed, turning away and

staring at the black hole that led deeper into the earth. "You left me at the end. I'll never forgive you for that."

"I didn't leave you," she said. "You just didn't come with me to the prayer." She raised her arm feebly. "We can do it again. This time we'll do it together. What do you say?" She choked. "I can't go on bleeding like this forever."

"If you go to her, you'll just black out," Frederick said.

Kara looked at the ceiling. The glaze across her eyes had thickened. Her warm brown irises were now cold and colorless. Yet she seemed to be looking far away and seeing clearly.

"I don't think so," she said.

"You're talking nonsense," Frederick said.

She looked at him. "Maybe."

"Kara," he said.

"Please come with me, Fred," she said.

He was suddenly confused, this all-powerful general who had laid waste to millions of lives. "But you hate my guts," he said.

She tried to smile. She didn't quite make it. She was in too much pain. "Yes," she said. "But I wish I didn't. And I wish you didn't hate me. Maybe that's the real reason the Illumni sent us back in time. For this wish." She bit her lip. I knew she tasted blood. It was now pouring out the side of her mouth. Her right lung must be drowning in it, I thought. "Will you come with me?" she asked.

Frederick appeared to forget me for a moment. He

knelt at Kara's side. "Nothing will change," he said. "You said it yourself. You're finished."

She nodded. "But what about us?"

The word startled him. "Us?"

She touched his cheek. "Us."

Frederick blinked. There could have been something in his eye. He didn't seem able to get it out.

"All right," he said. "I'll go with you to them. But your boyfriend is going to wait for us with a noose around his neck."

"I don't mind," I said.

Frederick had me lie down in the most uncomfortable position, flat on my belly with my arms behind my back. He tied my hands and feet together so that I was strung up like a bow. He kept his knife beside him the whole time he worked on the knots. He did an admirable job of choking off the blood supply through my wrists and ankles. He had probably been an outstanding Boy Scout as a child. But as he said, I was not in a position to make demands. I kept my mouth shut.

It was weird to see Frederick sit close to Kara and shut his eyes. It wasn't that he was in any physical danger from Kara or me, but in another sense he was placing himself in a vulnerable position. He would be opening himself up to feelings he hadn't felt in decades. Maybe he wasn't such a steel-hearted son of a bitch after all.

I didn't know what was going to happen. But if Becky did die and Kara didn't evaporate, I was going to have to get Kara to a hospital soon. I wondered what would happen if I took her to the same hospital where Becky was. The doctors would probably think they were seeing a ghost.

"Mark," Kara called softly, unable to raise her head and look at me. "I don't know if I should say goodbye."

"Don't," I said.

"Let's begin," Frederick interrupted, trying to make himself comfortable on the floor. He was too big to sit on a stone ledge. His expression was fixed in concentration. Briefly I saw the old general in his face: determined, cunning, burned out. Then his expression shifted in a less rigid direction and I imagined I saw Ray. But only for a moment. Then the breath seemed to leave his body, and his face became set like that of a dead person. The same thing happened to Kara. I let a few minutes go by. The tension was unbearable. I didn't know if, when Kara had left, her gunshot wound had closed the door behind her.

Then I noticed a sweet odor in the air. It reminded me of the first time I had visited the cave, the smell of a forest after a spring rain. But now it was stronger. It was almost as if the cave was attached to a corner of the paradise the Illumni had created on future earth. The fragrance was drifting out of the hole on the far side of the room. I took it to mean we were running out of time.

"Kara," I finally said.

"I am in the hospital," she replied after a brief pause. To my surprise, although her voice was still soft, it was clearer than it had been before she went into her trance. She sounded like Becky.

"How is Becky?" I asked.

"I am floating above her," Kara said. "She is unconscious."

"How can you speak if you're in her mind and she's unconscious?"

"She is floating above her body," Kara said.

The implications of Kara's comment took a minute to hit me. Becky was alive, but she was outside her body.

"What's happening?" I asked.

"There are wires hooked up to her," Kara said. "There are monitors. The top of her head is covered with a towel. There's blood. Becky is watching from the ceiling, watching her body. The doctors are watching—there's nothing anyone can do now. They've let Ray come into the room. They're talking to him. They tell him his girlfriend is going to die."

Kara fell silent. I checked on Frederick. His face was still flat and lifeless, but his right cheek had begun to twitch.

"What's Ray doing?" I asked Kara.

"He's sitting beside Becky," she said. "He's very pale. He keeps looking at a screen. It measures Becky's brain waves. The waves are almost flat. There is little brain activity." Kara paused. "Becky is worried about Ray."

"The Becky who is outside her body?" I asked.

"There is only one of us outside," Kara said. "There is only one of us. Ray is upset. I want to tell him I'm all right. I can't tell him. He is beginning to . . ."

201

Kara felt silent again. I was surprised to see Frederick had rolled onto his side. It was hard to believe, but he was slipping into the fetal position.

"He's beginning to cry?" I asked Kara.

"Yes," she said. "It's sad. Wait. Something has begun to beep."

"The monitor attached to her brain?"

"No," Kara said. "Another one. One attached to the heart. It's beeping. Ray is trying to get the doctors to do something. They don't want to. They tell Ray it's hopeless. Let her go. Ray is arguing with them. He is—oh, no."

"What?" I asked.

"He's shoved one of the doctors to the floor. But the man is OK. He gets up. He's not mad at Ray. He's a nice man. He understands. He tries to comfort Ray. I'm trying, too, but I can't. He can't hear me. I touch him and he can't feel me. He's so sad."

"Are you sad?"

"Only for him," she said.

Kara fell silent for a third time. The fragrant breeze blowing in through the black hole grew stronger. The smell was intoxicating. It made Kara's earlier description of the blue and red trees easy to imagine. Had the circumstances been less hellish, I could have believed heaven was near at hand. Kara spoke again.

"The monitor is beeping faster," she said. "The heart—the heart is going to stop!" Kara's whole body jumped. Her voice got loud and excited. "Tell him I am all right! Tell him I will see him again!"

"What's Ray doing?" I asked. Frederick had buried his face in the floor, but now his body was shaking, too.

"He's begging her not to leave him," Kara said. "He can't stand it. He's holding on to her. The doctors are trying to pull him away, but he won't let go. He's afraid no one's ever going to love him the way Becky loved him."

"Does Becky love him?" I asked.

Kara was long in answering. "Yes."

"Does he love Becky?"

"Oh, yes," she said. "He would give his life if she could go on living." Kara suddenly became very still. When she spoke next, her voice was faint. "The beeping has stopped."

Ten seconds went by. Twenty seconds. I counted them. I was praying. If Kara continued to live now that Becky was dead, it meant that my theory was correct, that the inside of the cave was unaffected by the laws of causality. When my count reached one hundred, Kara and Frederick opened their eyes together. Frederick sat up and dusted off his shirt. Kara strained to roll onto her side. She reached out to touch him. He turned and looked at first her hand, then her face. Their eyes met.

"It was horrible," she said.

"Yes," he said.

"It was beautiful," she said.

He touched her hand. The hard lines of the general's face were gone. "What did all these years do to us?" he asked.

"What we let them do," she said.

"Was that really us?"

"It was us."

He nodded. "I had forgotten how it used to be."

Kara smiled. "In the hospital I just wanted to tell you I was all right. Now I can."

He gestured to her wound. "Can I do anything for you?"

"Yes," she said. "Kiss me goodbye."

He kissed her. I couldn't help but watch. My eyes were damp. When Frederick was done, he stood and took out his knife.

"I suppose I owe you one, Forum," he said.

"Think nothing of it," I said, knowing he had not taken out the blade to threaten me.

He knelt by my side and cut the rope. I couldn't get over the change in him. He looked twenty years younger. Of course he was in a body that was only twenty years old. He offered me his hand when he was through setting me free.

"You have guts," he said. "I think we could have been friends."

I shook his hand firmly. "Maybe we will be."

He understood. "Don't tell him about me."

"I won't," I promised.

Frederick stood. He turned to Kara. "I came out seconds behind you and Vincent. You didn't know that, did you?"

"I didn't," Kara said.

He looked at his watch. "I have to go now." He turned away.

"Ray," Kara called.

He stopped. "Yes?"

"You're my favorite general," she said.

He smiled faintly. Then he nodded in my direction and turned and disappeared into the black hole. I wasn't sure where he was going, but I knew it would be foolish to try to follow him. I hurried to Kara's side.

"You're alive," I exclaimed.

Kara was staring at the spot where her husband had vanished. "Not for long," she said.

"That's not true. Don't you understand? Becky is dead, but you're not. Time has let you slip by. I'll get you to a hospital." I slipped my arms under her. "You're going to make it."

She stopped me. "Becky's not dead."

"What? You said her heart stopped."

"It did."

"Did the doctors restart it?"

"No," Kara said. "They couldn't if they tried. But her brain is still alive."

I understood what she was saying. Even when all respiration halted, the brain still took five to ten minutes to actually be destroyed.

"Where is she now?" I asked.

"She's still floating above her body."

"Will she leave when everything inside it is dead?"

Kara finally looked at me. "When I join her."

I shook my head. "No. You're going to stay in this cave. This is where the Illumni put their time machine. Becky's death won't affect you. You'll go right on living. Then I'll take you to the hospital."

Kara was sad for me. ''Mark, this cave is just a cave. There is no time machine.''

''What do you mean?''

Fighting against her pain, she tried to sit up. ''Take me outside.''

''No! The laws of causality don't apply in here. You're not going outside. I won't let you.''

Kara touched my cheek. Even hurt as she was, she was so beautiful. I remembered the first time I had ever seen her, when I walked into the record store. She had been so full of life.

''Please,'' she said. ''I want to see the moon before I go.''

Tears filled my eyes. I closed them and the tears welled over my cheeks. I could bear anything, I thought. Even the end of the world. But this was too much. My heart was breaking—physically, I could feel it tearing apart inside me. How could the Illumni do this to me? How could they take both Kara and Becky?

''No,'' I moaned.

She cupped my face in both her hands. ''Look at me, Mark. Who do you see?''

I did as I was told. ''Becky.''

''Who else?''

''Kara.''

She smiled. ''And someone else.''

''Who?''

''Take me outside,'' she said. ''I will show you.''

I lifted her carefully. I had thought her light before; now I could scarcely feel her body in my arms. It was difficult even to focus on her, as if she were somehow becoming transparent. But I might have imagined this. Quickly I carried her from the cave and out onto the path. The moon was now directly overhead and surrounded with a wide white halo. Her right arm hung around my neck. With her left arm she pointed to the moon.

"See," she said.

"What?"

"There's the moon. There's me."

"So?" I said.

Kara snuggled against my cheek. "It feels so good to hold you. It's like holding Vincent. I was never afraid when he was with me. I'm not afraid now."

"Why did I choose that name—Vincent?"

"The forest where I met you again after all those years looked like a Vincent van Gogh painting. The colors were so vibrant." She smiled to herself. "I chose the name for you, Mark. It was a good name."

"I always liked it—Chaneen."

"So I'm the queen of the universe at last," she said, pleased.

"You have always been my queen. Can't I take you to the hospital?"

"I am at the hospital. I'm floating in the same way the moon floats in the sky."

"I don't understand."

"It doesn't matter," she said. "It's not your time yet. That won't be for a long time. I love you, Mark.

In the years to come, you must never forget that. Don't be sad, and you'll live forever." Kara kissed me gently on the lips. She hugged me tight. "I love you more than the sun and the moon put together."

"Even with my lousy clothes?"

She smiled. "Look at the moon and close your eyes, Mark. Don't let go of me."

I turned my gaze. The moon was so bright. Even when I shut my eyes, I could still see an impression of it in my mind. An impression that went deep, like the last thought at the time of death. It grew in both size and brilliance as I focused on it. Soon it was as bright as the real moon outside my body, **brigh**ter even, and I almost forgot the real one for a moment. But then I opened my eyes and lowered my head. And I was standing alone on the outside. And Kara was gone.

Ten years have gone by since that night. A lot has changed. A lot has remained the same. I don't know if that's good or bad. I'm twenty-nine years old now. Before I can talk about the last ten years, though, I must finish with that night and the following day.

I went back to my apartment. I had to hitchhike home. The Ferrari I had driven to the cave was gone. At the apartment, Vincent's black Ferrari was also gone. I could understand why, sort of. Becky was dead. There was no Kara in the future to come back in time and buy the cars. Consequently, they were never bought. I just thought they were because I had a good memory. But then again, at least one of them must have been bought. One of them *had* killed Becky. But who had killed Becky? Kara? She couldn't have because if she had then she wouldn't have been alive to kill her. On the other hand, Kara must have killed her because no one else did.

The logic got awfully sticky, and it only got worse the longer I thought about it. Nevertheless, I will give my thoughts on the matter after I deal with the official investigation into Becky's death.

The next morning I heard a knock at my door—exactly as I had the previous morning. This time, however, I didn't yell for the person to come in. I got up and put on my pants. It was a good thing I did. It was the police. Apparently Becky had talked to Ray about the computer games I wrote. The police had contacted my software company, and they had given the police my address. Now the police wanted to talk to me. It seemed they were getting conflicting stories about what had happened the night before. They offered me a ride to the station. I took it and wondered if they would give me a ride home.

Ray and Ted were at the station. Both looked awful. I was surprised to learn they had been arrested. Actually, I could understand why they had arrested Ted. The police had probably taken one look at his stoned expression and figured they'd found the pipeline—or rather, the bloodstream—for half the Colombian cocaine in southern California. But I had to sit down when I learned Ray had been arrested for manslaughter.

The detective in charge of the case was old and tough. His thin hair was as white as his starched shirt, his red face wrinkled and cracked from the sun. He held his spine ramrod straight and when he shook my hand he hurt my little finger. He looked and talked like a cop, and had I been told he had shot a few people in the line of duty, I would have assumed they were teenagers. He gave me a dirty look as I sat down. His name was Lieutenant Cocker.

"Were you at the scene of the crime last night, Mr. Forum?" he asked, wasting no time on small talk.

"What crime is that?" I asked innocently. I needed information. I didn't know how Ted and Ray's stories were in conflict. Ted sat to my right, Ray to my left. Lieutenant Cocker pointed to Ray.

"I've already told you," the lieutenant said. "This young man has been arrested on a charge of man-slaughter. Are you saying he's innocent?"

I had to move carefully. "Who's accusing him of killing Becky?"

"I am," Ted spoke up. I turned toward him.

"Did you see him run over Becky?" I asked, grateful that the detective hadn't tried to get my story in private. I could only assume I wasn't under suspicion.

"No," Ted said. "But he was there."

"What about me?" I asked. "I was there."

"But you were on foot," Ted said quickly, taken aback by my remark. "Ray was the only one who had his car there."

"How did you arrive at the mall?" Lieutenant Cocker interrupted.

"I went there with Becky," I said. "We were in her car."

Lieutenant Cocker nodded impatiently. "We found Becky's car parked on the other side of the mall from where she was run down. But what are you stalling for? Tell me what went on last night."

I was reluctant to speak when I wasn't sure if Ted's

obvious memory loss was a result of cosmic causality or simply dead brain cells.

"I don't understand what you're asking me," I said. "How does Ray's story conflict with Ted's?"

Ray had been sitting quietly with his head bowed. Now he sat up angrily. "What the hell are you talking about?" he demanded. "You saw what happened, Mark. That Kara bitch ran Becky down in her red Ferrari."

"What red Ferrari?" Ted asked.

"The one with the headlights that were shining on the two girls!" Ray snapped. "Christ, how wasted were you last night, Ted? The car was sitting right in front of your eyes."

"What two girls?" Ted asked. "Becky was the only girl there."

"When you got there," Ray said, making a vain effort at a patient tone, "Kara was lying on the ground beside Becky. They were both bleeding."

"Why was this Kara also bleeding?" Lieutenant Cocker asked.

Ray glanced at me and lowered his head. "I don't know."

"There was only one puddle of blood on the ground," Cocker said. "What do you have to say about that?"

"Nothing," Ray replied, clearly confused.

At last I thought I understood. Causality *was* at work, but in a strangely limited fashion. Only the three of us in the present—Becky, Ray, and I—could remember the true sequence of events in which our future selves were involved. Otherwise, to other people, Kara, Frederick, and Vincent hadn't even existed.

"I'll tell you what happened," I said to the detective. "I saw it all. Becky and I were walking across the parking lot. Ray had just gotten off work. He was over by his car. We were trying to catch up with him. Then this other car came out of nowhere. It hit Becky and drove off. Ray didn't have anything to do with it."

Ted frowned. "But Ray was beating you up," he said.

"That's ridiculous," I said. "He was just upset. We all were. We weren't fighting."

"But what about Kara?" Ray asked. "Becky's twin sister?"

"Becky doesn't have a sister," I said.

"Yeah, she does," Ray said indignantly. "The girl looked just like her."

"We've spoken to Becky's parents," Lieutenant Cocker said dryly. "There is no sister."

Ray was ready to throw a fit. "But I went out with this girl on a date!" he shouted.

"Why would you go out with your girlfriend's sister on a date?" Cocker asked.

"I didn't know it was her sister," Ray said.

"But you just said this Kara looked like Becky," Cocker said.

"She did," Ray said. "I just didn't notice it at first."

"Lieutenant," I said reasonably, "this whole experience has the three of us in a state of shock. Ted and I were good friends of Becky's, but Ray was the closest to her. They'd been going together a long time, and suddenly she was lying on the ground dying. You can see how he could begin to have hallucinations.''

"But Kara came into my store!" Ray cried. "She came in with you!"

"I think if you check with Becky's parents," I said to Cocker, ignoring Ray for the moment, "you will discover that Becky's first name is Kara."

"It is?" Ray asked.

"They already told me that," Cocker said, unimpressed. He eyed the three of us suspiciously. "But I still don't buy how all your stories could vary so much." He gestured to Ted. "What do you have to say about Forum's version of what happened last night?"

"It sounds good," Ted replied cautiously.

"Is it true?" Cocker asked.

"I told you," Ted said. "I wasn't actually there when Becky got hit. It just looked like Ray had done it."

"Why?" Cocker insisted.

Ted searched his memory and appeared to get lost. "He was carrying something. It made me think he—I don't know."

"What was he carrying?" Cocker pressed.

Ray was watching Ted intently. He was worried. Only I knew that Ted was remembering the ghost of the gun that wasn't there. Already I could see my theory would have to be modified. Maybe nobody else was going to remember Kara and Vincent and Frederick, but their shadows were inside a few heads somewhere. Ted had seen Ray and me fighting for the

214

gun that the future Ray wasn't going to be coming back in time to give Ray.

"It could have been a gun," Ted replied.

"Did you see a gun?" Cocker asked.

"No," Ted said.

"Were you carrying a gun?" Cocker asked Ray.

Ray hesitated. He glanced at me. "No," he said finally.

Lieutenant Cocker sighed. "I should lock the three of you up and let you sit for a week and then see what you have to say." He pointed at Ted. "I'm letting you go by the kind permission of the letter of the law. My men were there to investigate a hit-and-run, not to search for drugs. But I think you'll find that you are now unemployed and that the paraphernalia you kept at the mall has gone up in smoke. You are free to go. I don't want to see you back here anytime soon."

Ted got up and fairly ran from the room. Lieutenant Cocker was not through. He stood up from his desk and walked behind us. Ray sweated out the move. But I figured, what the hell. The evidence Cocker needed to convict either of us had never existed. Not now, anyway.

"Both of you are lying to me," Cocker said. "You're a lot better at it, Forum, than Mr. Gardener here, but you're not good enough. Now I want to know what happened last night, and I want to know the truth."

"Are you placing me under arrest?" I asked.

"Not yet," Cocker said.

"If you were to arrest me, what would the charge be?" I asked.

"Obstructing justice. Possible manslaughter."

"No one's saying I hit Becky," I said.

"Don't fool with me, Forum," Cocker snapped.

I decided he was trying to intimidate me. "I already told you the truth," I said. "A car came out of nowhere and hit Becky and drove off."

"And you have no idea what type of car it was or what the driver looked like?" he asked.

"Absolutely none," I said, throwing a look Ray's way. "It was dark, wasn't it, Ray?"

Ray held my eye for a moment, "Yeah," he said slowly. "It was pitch-black. Neither of us saw a thing."

Cocker chewed on that for a minute. "And now you're agreeing with Forum, is that it, Gardener?" he asked.

Ray nodded. "Looks like it."

"Get the hell out of here, both of you," Cocker said, moving back to his desk. "But just know one thing. If I find the tiniest bit of evidence that could be used to nail either of your asses, I'm going to go out and buy myself a big hammer. Do you get my drift?"

We both told him that we did. Ray followed me down the long hallway that led out of the police station. He didn't speak until we were standing in the parking lot beside his car. His grief was with him still. The circles under his eyes were dark and deep.

"What gives, Mark?" he asked.

"I can't tell you," I said. I raised my hand as he started to protest. "If I did tell you, you wouldn't believe me. Trust me."

"Why should I trust you? Becky died last night. She's dead. I can't believe I'm saying it, but it's true." He put his hand to his head to steady himself. His skin was pale and damp. "I can't take this," he moaned. "The whole world's gone insane."

I put my hand on his arm. "You felt that way last night when her heart stopped. You felt so upset that you had to lash out at something, anything. You pushed a doctor to the floor."

He stared at me in amazement. "Who told you that?"

"Becky. She told me something else. That she was all right."

"When?"

"When she died."

"What are you talking about?" he asked.

"Magic. I know that sounds foolish, but I can't explain it any other way. Just know that before Becky left she wanted you to know that she was all right and that you were her favorite general."

A strange light touched Ray's face. "She used to tell me that I would be a general one day," he said.

"Then you will be. She was a special girl. She and Kara both were. You weren't hallucinating. Kara was real. Her hitting Becky was just an accident."

"I know," he said. "She was trying to hit me."

"Because she thought you were guilty of something that you hadn't done." I let go of his arm. "You'll be able to take it better the next time."

"The next time what?" he asked.

"The next time the whole world goes insane," I said. "You'll know not to lash out like you did at the doctor. I have faith in you, Ray."

217

He gave me an incredulous look and then shook his head. "You're crazy, you know that, Mark?"

"So are you," I said. "I wonder what Becky saw in either of us."

Ray offered me a ride home. I took it. He shook my hand as he dropped me at my apartment building. He promised to keep in touch. Maybe he forgot, I don't know. I never saw him again.

But I don't think he ever forgot Becky. Or what it was like to hold her in his arms and watch her die. For the sake of the world, I hope not.

My life went on. I never went back to Becky's record store. I never stood at the door and glanced over my shoulder and imagined I saw a guy with pale blond hair holding one of my computer games. I seldom dreamed of Vincent and Kara. I remembered them—that was enough. My programming skills improved dramatically, particularly my graphics. I copied Vincent's style. It came easy to me. I didn't consider it plagiarism. I started to make good money, and by my twenty-second birthday I was making great money. I wrote a program called "Decision" then. The reason I waited three years to write it was so that the industry could develop computers with RAMs big enough to hold the game's many complexities.

The game was an instant success. In fact, it became so big that I gained celebrity status. The major talk shows wanted me as a guest. The game was talked about in high schools and colleges across the country. The first nonviolent video game, it was called. Teachers used it to teach nuclear age morality. Kids played it even though they knew they couldn't win. Privately, I found it all very amusing. I just didn't see myself as a modern-day prophet. I cashed my royalty checks and stayed out of the limelight.

With my newfound wealth I was in a position to see the finest heart surgeons in the world. But I never made an appointment. The more I thought about the Illumni's comment on health and happiness, the more profound it seemed. Maybe I was just afraid of dying on the operating table, I don't know. I'd still wake up in the middle of the night with pain in my chest, but I stopped feeling sorry for myself, or feeling unloved, which I think is the same thing.

I lived alone, as I had always lived alone. Occasionally I dated different girls, but I knew nothing would ever come of it. That is the problem with finding the perfect girl. You can't find her twice. That is not to say that Kara was without her faults. No one knew them better than I. Except perhaps Vincent, whom I miss as much as Kara. I think about him a lot. He was so kind, so at peace. I ask myself who he really was. I mean, I know he was me, but *which* me was he? It may seem a silly way to put the question, yet I wonder if it is not *the* question.

You see, I think Vincent had no faults. None.

Ten years later I'm still trying to understand what happened.

Kara talked about superior beings from another planet. I could see how she thought that. She was in outer space when bright lights suddenly swept in and rescued everybody. But from that point on, her story was filled with one inconsistency and coincidence after another, and I don't think she even realized it.

Several I brought up at the time of her explanation. The Illumni supposedly had no bodies, but they needed spaceships to get around and had gender distinctions. She only communicated with one, and that one happened to be female.. The Illumni took a single spot on earth and turned it into a virtual paradise, and that spot just happened to be where Kara grew up. Given Kara's basic premise of a highly advanced alien culture, none of this is impossible, but it makes me wonder if she wasn't missing the sun because it was so bright. What I mean is, the truth might have been so overwhelming and yet so simple that it just escaped her.

Several points puzzle me. One is that I, as Vincent, wasn't even on the space station—much less alive— and yet I was able to come back in time. Kara explained this away by saying that I had been frozen and stored in ice above the Arctic Circle, where no atomic bombs exploded. At the time it all sounded awfully convenient to me. Why was I the only one who was thawed out? How exactly did the Illumni bring me back to life? They weren't God. They were supposed to just be friendly aliens.

I think Kara was wrong. I think the Popsicle Mark Forum Theory was given to her or perhaps created by her. Not intentionally to mislead her, but to give her a framework from which to interpret certain events that couldn't be understood unless the Big Thing was understood first. In other words, I think Kara missed something important the moment the Illumni showed up, and because she missed that, nothing she said about subsequent events can be accepted as truth.

What exactly was going on with Kara and Frederick when the Illumni appeared? They were dying. Then suddenly, miraculously, a bright light came to their rescue. No, not just one bright light—about a hundred bright lights. One for every person on the space station. I find that an amazing coincidence. An alien space ship filled with the exact number of aliens to personally attend to each dying crew member of an American space station.

From the start, something about the description of the Illumni reminded me of something I had read about in magazines and books. A bright white light. A peace beyond description. People who suffer a near-death experience talk about things like that. There have been dozens of shows on TV about it. People get in car accidents or almost drown or get hit by lightning, and suddenly they're thrust into a realm of blissful light where their lives are reviewed so they can see where they've done well and where they've screwed up. Granted, Kara didn't exactly describe this, but the parallel is striking. In fact, it's almost unnerving.

Who were the Illumni? *What* were they?

I realize I'm treading into the area of philosophical speculation, and believe me, I have no desire to do so. I know I will only get lost. Nevertheless, I'm willing to go a little further, with the understanding that I will not be arriving at any definite conclusions. I'm not an Einstein who can think in six dimensions at once. I'm just a survivor of strange times. In a sense, I am also a survivor of death.

I was in Vincent's body. Frederick cut Vincent's

throat. Then I reviewed my entire life, even the end of it, while I simultaneously experienced the end of Vincent's life. It was the most horrible thing to go through, yet it eventually brought me to a place of wonderful joy. In the end, before Kara called me back, I went into a bright light. I *was* the bright light. There was no difference. There was only one. Then I saw the space station. Yes, it's true I responded to Kara when she called to me. The question is, to *which* Kara did I respond? The one waiting by my side in the cave?

Or the one dying aboard the space station?

This is getting confusing. Let me just say what I think and be done with it. I'll phrase it in the form of another question. If one version of our future selves could come back in time, why couldn't an even more distant future version also come back?

Who was Vincent? I think he was one of the Illumni.

Who were the Illumni? I think they are ourselves.

I think Vincent was myself from a far more distant future than even Kara could dream of. I also think he was that part of me that exists in the dimension beyond life. I realize these statements appear to support entirely separate points of view. But do they really? I was dead when Kara wished me back to life. I had been dead for close to thirty years. And suddenly I was up and walking around in a flower-strewn meadow that sounded suspiciously closer to heaven than to Los Angeles on the best of days. Then what did I do? As Vincent, I went back in time with a girl who was anxious to change her past so her future could also be changed. But as Vincent, I didn't sweat a thing. I didn't interfere because I knew that what was to be would be.

Several other points lead me to believe Vincent was no ordinary time traveler. Kara said repeatedly how highly developed Vincent's mind was, and I could see that for myself. When Becky glimpsed Vincent—via Kara's memories—she saw him lit up like a light bulb. In the same vision, Becky said it was Vincent, and Vincent alone, who possessed telepathic powers. Also, and perhaps most important, before she ran out the door to her death, Becky said I was not real. Still caught in a portion of her trance, I think she had mistaken me for Vincent. And in that trance, I don't think Vincent was a flesh-and-blood creature.

Of course, it could be argued that Becky should have been able to see Vincent only as Kara remembered him. Nevertheless, Becky's remarks, made in a state of complete ignorance of the travel experiment, may have been more accurate than anything Kara told me.

What's the main problem with time travel? Causality? The paradox of going back in time and killing your grandmother is a piece of cake compared to the problem of immortality. We have bodies. They are supposed to wear out and eventually stop working. But if you've got a time machine, and if you're careful, you never have to die. Yet just before Kara died, she said there was no time machine. In fact, by her tone, she implied that there had *never* been a time machine. The cave was just a cave, she said. I think she was right. *I think, in the end, Kara understood precisely what I am talking about right now.* She

223

pointed to the moon. To the white light. That's me, she said. And she was happy.

Who were the Illumni? Vincent once referred to them as angels.

I'm sorry. This analysis will have to be left incomplete. I'm getting tired. It's late, very late. My time has finally come. The night I saw as the end of my life has arrived. I'm sitting at my table on the side of the hill. The moon is out. It's bright—it's a full moon. I have my gas lantern nearby. The orange flame burns without flickering beneath the glass cover. I warm my hands above it. My fingers shake, although the night is warm. I'm trying to finish my story. It's not easy. I know I shouldn't complain, but I'm having chest pain. It comes in waves, like my memories of Kara and Vincent.

I still don't understand why things happen the way they do. I wish this story could have been a happy story with a happy ending. I did not want Becky and Kara to die. At funerals, ministers often say we're only here for a short time before God calls us back home to heaven. Perhaps they, too—like Kara—have it backward. Perhaps we're never really here when we're born, and we never really leave when we die. That makes sense if there's time travel. If I had a time machine, I could keep pushing the buttons and go around and around the calendar like the stars in the sky. I could live forever, but maybe then I would never get anywhere. I would only become a dream of what I could have been, a shadow of who Vincent will be.

I don't want to die. In spite of all I've been through,

death still frightens me. I'm alone. I wish Kara were here. If my heart should suddenly stop, there'll be no one to freeze my body to keep it for the day it could be revived. That's another reason I don't believe everything is the way I was led to believe. As far as I know, there is still no way to keep water from expanding when it turns to ice. Not that I blame Kara. I feel nothing but gratitude for her.

The city appears very peaceful from where I sit. Bathed in the light of the moon, it looks like a surreal black-and-white painting that I would gladly hang on my bedroom wall and look at each night before retiring to pleasant dreams. But I know it will not always be this way. Tonight I'm worrying about myself, but I can honestly say that I usually think more about what's to become of the world. Unfortunately, of all the many incidents that Kara predicted, the one thing that rang terribly true was the impending cataclysm. I see it in the headlines of the newspapers. I hear it in the voices of the politicians. But I'm not without hope. I can close my eyes and sit so still that the outside voices all but disappear. Then I see and hear something quite different. A hundred white angels flying quietly through the nighttime streets, stopping at a house here, an apartment there, and whispering into the ears of their sleeping counterparts, "Wake up. Wake up. The moon is in the sky."

I have to put down my pen. I have to close my eyes. The pain in my chest is getting worse. Perhaps I have not remembered my love as well as I should have. It is not easy to stay happy living on memories alone. My heart is tired. It needs to rest.

But I'm not going to burn this manuscript, as I burned the one before. This time I have not come to the end in despair.

I feel Vincent near me. I sense Kara. They come to me from another time and place, where there is only happiness. I feel as if two angels stand behind me and touch my head. It may be only my imagination, but I do not think so. They are real, like my story, although these two do not whisper to me. They stand silent. They have already told me all there is to tell.

I know I will see a light when the dawn finally comes. The cool white light of the moon, shining forever in a starry universe that goes on forever, or the warm light of the sun, burning brilliantly in a sky all its own, a sky that lasts only a day.

I know I will either live or die.

I wish I could say which it will be.

Look for Christopher Pike's
Witch

Available as an Archway book

Christopher Pike's long-awaited
adult novel
Sati
Now available in hardcover

About the Author

CHRISTOPHER PIKE was born in Brooklyn, New York, but grew up in Los Angeles, where he lives to this day. Prior to becoming a writer, he worked in a factory, painted houses, and programmed computers. His hobbies include astronomy, meditating, running, playing with his nieces and nephews, and making sure his books are prominently displayed in local bookstores. He is the author of *Last Act, Spellbound, Gimme a Kiss, Remember Me, Scavenger Hunt, Final Friends* 1, 2, and 3, and *Fall into Darkness,* all available from Pocket Books. *Slumber Party, Weekend, Chain Letter, The Tachyon Web,* and *Sati*—an adult novel about a very unusual lady—are also by Mr. Pike.

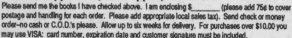
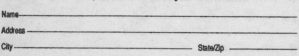